Secrets of Sugarcreek
+

SEARCHING

for

Samuel

Secrets of Sugarcreek

SEARCHING *for* Samuel

SERENA B. MILLER

Edited by
HANNAH MILLER

LJ EMORY
PUBLISHING

"Love always protects, always trusts,
always hopes, always perseveres.
Love never fails."

~ *1 Corinthians 13:7-8 (NIV)*

To my Amish friend, Esther,
whose strength and laughter brought light
into my home during a difficult time.

CHAPTER 1

The horse knew something was wrong before I did.

From my seat on the porch, I saw King—our lead Belgian—suddenly throw up his massive head and stop dead in his traces. His ears pricked toward our long gravel driveway. My Amish farm manager, Lucas Hershberger, stood still—his hands gripping the wooden plow handles as he listened.

Then I heard it. A drumming of hooves, urgent and fast, shattering the usual morning calm. A black buggy careened around the bend, its wheels spitting gravel. The horse pulling it was lathered in sweat, its sides heaving.

A young woman was at the reins, her voice carrying across the yard. *"Lucas! Komm schnell!"*

Something about the raw desperation in her voice sent a prickle down my spine.

Trouble rarely announced itself so boldly among the rolling hills and whispered prayers of the quiet farming community of Sugarcreek, Ohio. I had been lost in the book I was writing, but now my fingers froze above the keyboard. I hit save and jumped to my feet.

The buggy jolted to a stop, and the woman vaulted out, hitting the ground running. Her dark dress whipped around her legs, her white prayer *kapp* askew.

Lucas anchored the plow, secured the reins, and ran to meet her. When they met in the middle of the field, she grabbed the front of his blue shirt with both hands, speaking rapidly in Pennsylvania Dutch—her voice sharp and loud with panic.

In the buggy, a little girl—no more than ten—climbed into the front seat, took the reins, and murmured soothingly to the skittish horse.

Two younger girls followed her to the front and huddled together beside their sister, their wide eyes locked on their mother.

I hesitated on the porch, torn between my ingrained New York City instinct to mind my own business and the growing urge to help. Here in Sugarcreek, people either ran toward trouble to lend a hand or popped a casserole into the oven to deliver later. The one thing you did not do, if you wanted to be part of this community, was nothing.

Since I very much wanted to be part of this community, I closed my laptop and stepped down off the porch to help with the children.

I recognized the woman now. Gretchen. Lucas's younger sister. I met her when she and her husband, Samuel, came to get a pony Lucas had found that was gentle enough for their three little daughters.

As I crossed the yard, I mentally inventoried my kitchen to see what I could offer. In Amish country, offering food and drink was as instinctive as breathing. It was the first act of comfort, no matter what calamity had struck.

"Excuse me," I said, approaching Lucas and Gretchen. "I have cookies and lemonade at the house if the children would like to come inside."

The girls, all dressed in matching light blue dresses, turned toward me, their faces as expectant as little sunflowers. They did not clamor or beg. I had not yet met an Amish child who did. Lucas's gaze met mine, his blue eyes worried and distant, as if he'd forgotten I existed. Whatever news Gretchen had brought had shaken him.

Then his expression softened. I hoped it was from relief at knowing someone else was here to help shoulder the burden.

"*Danki*, Amy," he said, his voice steady with the quiet authority most Amish men carried naturally. "*Die kinner* would appreciate it. But keep them on the porch where they can see their mother."

Gretchen released her grip on her brother's shirt and turned to her daughters. "*Geh mit der Amy, meedlies. Sei brav.*"

I glanced at Lucas for translation.

"My sister told them to go with you and to be good," he said.

The girls climbed down from the buggy, but the eldest first led the buggy horse to the trough and watched it drink. I was impressed with her sense of responsibility and self-confidence. She knew the horse needed tending, even if the adults were too busy having a crisis to notice. Only after she'd tied the horse to the hitching post did she take her sisters' hands and accompany me to the porch.

Although their hair was in braids, none of them wore the traditional prayer *kapp*. Their mother must have been terribly distracted to have ignored that. They were also barefoot, but that was normal. I winced when I saw them walking across the graveled driveway with their little bare feet, but they didn't seem to notice. Like most Amish children, they were used to almost always going barefoot.

I seated them at the picnic table on the porch, and they waited patiently as I brought a plate of sugar cookies out, along with lemonade in paper cups.

"*Danki*," they chorused politely, daintily selecting one cookie each.

"My name is Amy," I said, settling across from them.

The oldest girl spoke for her sisters. "I am Sarah," then gestured to the others. "This is Ruth. She's five. And our baby sister is Laura. She's three."

"I'm glad to have you visiting."

"What is that?" Sarah pointed to my laptop, which I'd left sitting on an old table where I liked to write on nice days.

"It's my computer."

"What is it for?"

"It is used for many things, but I write stories on it."

Sarah was less interested in the computer than the story-telling part.

"What kind of stories?"

"People hire me to write stories about their lives."

Sarah stared at me for a good three seconds, as though examining each of my words. Then she said, "I tell stories to my sisters sometimes when they won't go to sleep."

"I imagine they are wonderful stories."

"Probably they are not," she said. "My sisters go to sleep quickly when I start."

Laura gulped down her lemonade in a few swallows and held out her cup for more.

Sarah gave what sounded like a reprimand in Pennsylvania Dutch. "*Nimm net zu viel!*"

"What did you say?" I asked.

"I told her not to drink so much."

"There's plenty," I assured her, refilling Laura's cup.

Sarah hesitated. "But Laura cannot always wait."

"Wait for what?"

"She is not long out of diapers. If she drinks too much, she wets herself."

The quiet confession hung between us. A child burdened with a mother's worries.

"If anyone needs the bathroom, it's just inside," I offered. "You're welcome to use it."

Sarah nodded solemnly. "*Danki.*"

I changed the subject. "Is everything okay with your mother?"

"No." Sarah picked at her cookie. "Nothing is okay right now."

"Are you allowed to tell me why?"

She considered. "Our *Daett* is gone. *Mamm* doesn't know where he went."

Samuel was gone? No wonder Gretchen was distraught.

Little Laura reached for another cookie but glanced first to see if it would be approved by her older sister. Sarah nodded, and Laura snatched one up before her sister could change her mind. A few cookie crumbs clung to the sides of her tiny mouth.

"Has your mother called the police?"

"No." Sarah wiped Laura's mouth with a napkin.

I would have loved to ask why, but I had already asked too much. It was not kind to interrogate children.

"I hope your father comes back soon," I said. "Please help yourself to more cookies."

I saw Lucas and Gretchen approaching, his hand on her elbow—a rare display of touch among the Amish. Gretchen forced a smile as she stepped onto the porch. "*Ach,* look at this *gude* party!"

Lucas met my eyes. "Can I speak with you inside?"

"Of course."

I could feel the children's worried eyes on me as Lucas and I stepped into the kitchen. I hoped he could help them. I knew one thing for certain—Lucas would do everything he could.

CHAPTER 2

"What's going on?" I asked, as we stood beside the kitchen table.

Lucas exhaled slowly, as if gathering his thoughts. "Gretchen's husband has disappeared. She does not know where he is."

"How long has he been gone?"

"Since yesterday morning."

I frowned. "That doesn't seem long enough to cause such a panic."

"It does if one's husband is a thoughtful man who is rarely late for dinner."

The quiet certainty in his voice gave me pause. Where I came from, sometimes people disappeared for days, with no one raising an eyebrow. But here, in this close-knit community, a single missed meal was cause for alarm.

"Where does he work?" I asked, watching Lucas's troubled expression.

"At the sawmill, about two miles away." His fingers drummed once against the kitchen table. "He rode off on his bike yesterday morning and never returned. At first, Gretchen assumed he was working late to fill an order, which had happened once before. She put the girls to bed and slept in their room. Laura had a stomachache, and she wanted to be nearby."

I could hear Gretchen talking with her daughters outside. The thought of the fear she must be dealing with right now made my heart ache with sympathy.

"When she awoke this morning and realized Samuel still wasn't home, she panicked and drove the buggy to the mill." Lucas's voice grew tighter. "They told her he never came to work yesterday. That's when she went to his parents' home, hoping he'd spent the night there. His father has been ill, and Samuel checks on him daily, but they had not seen or heard from him either. That's when she came here."

"What does she want you to do?"

"Whatever I can," Lucas said. "I'm her older brother. She has always turned to me for help."

I mulled that over. What must it be like to have a brother to lean on? I could hardly imagine such a simple luxury. My family tree was more of a stunted shrub—just me and my mother, Desiree Stanton, an A-list actress who breezed into my life from time to time.

"Did they have a fight, perhaps?" The morning sunlight streamed through the kitchen window. It felt wrong to have such gorgeous spring weather when people I cared about were struggling.

Lucas shook his head. "She says they didn't, and I believe her." He walked to the window and gazed out. "Samuel is a gentle soul, and so is Gretchen. I doubt they've ever had a serious disagreement—let alone one bad enough for him to vanish without a word."

"She's certain he hasn't tried to call?" I asked. "Your people aren't always the easiest to reach."

"They have a phone booth at the end of their driveway with an answering machine. She checked before going to the mill. No messages." His concern was visible in the tightness around his eyes. "She's right to be worried. Samuel isn't the kind of man who disappears."

"Then why didn't she go to the police instead of you?"

Lucas turned from the window, his expression guarded. "We've learned over the years that the less we involve the *Englisch* in our lives, the better."

That stung. "Did you forget that I'm *Englisch*, Lucas?"

"I did not forget." The words hung between us, softened only by the gentleness in his voice.

Sometimes, Lucas could be a little too honest. His words contained no malice, but they still hurt, a reminder of the invisible line that separated his world from mine. I turned away, busying myself with rinsing a mug that had been sitting near the sink.

"The police have more resources to find Samuel." I tried to keep my voice neutral.

"Not necessarily," Lucas said. "He has no driver's license, no credit cards, no cell phone. There's little for them to trace. Our Amish grapevine may be a better tool—if we can get the word out quickly."

"Fair point," I admitted, turning to face him. "How can I help?"

"I need to check with relatives and friends who might have seen him. A car would be faster than a horse. Could you drive me?"

I hesitated. The clock on the wall ticked loudly in the silence. I had hours of research and writing scheduled for today. The deadline for my current project loomed like a storm cloud on the horizon.

But across from me stood Lucas, asking for help I could easily give.

"Of course I'll drive you," I said, reaching for my car keys. "Just point me in the right direction."

The look of gratitude Lucas gave me made me forget all about deadlines.

We stepped onto the porch, where Gretchen sat, holding herself together for the sake of her children. Laura snuggled against her, sucking her thumb. Ruth, unfazed, was finishing another cookie. Sarah looked worried, her young eyes too grave as she watched her mother.

"Take the girls home," Lucas told his sister. "Amy is taking me to speak with Samuel's friends and family to find out if they know anything."

If I were in Gretchen's place, I'd have insisted on coming along. But she'd been raised in a different culture. Her brother had spoken, and she accepted his decision. Instead of arguing, she gathered up the cups and plates, brushing away crumbs with steady hands that belied her distress.

"Please," I said. "That can wait. I'll take care of it later. Take your children home. The sooner we leave, the sooner we find your husband."

She shot me a grateful glance before gathering her daughters. Lucas unhitched the horses, leading them to pasture with practiced ease. His plow stood abandoned in the field, no doubt in the hope he'd soon return. I packed up my laptop and notes. If I had to wait in the car at some point, maybe I could still get a bit of writing done.

I'm a ghost writer by profession, but since moving to Sugarcreek, I've stopped telling people that. When people hear it, they sometimes think I write ghost stories, and the Amish do not approve of ghost stories. Nor do they approve of romances, thrillers, mysteries, or pretty much fiction of any kind.

At least I didn't need to change clothes to drive Lucas around today. Back in New York, I'd often worked in my pajamas, but once I inherited this farm from my ex-stepfather, I quickly learned that wasn't an option here. The Amish rose early, and they didn't believe in waiting for a decent hour to drop by. If they found you still in pajamas past seven o'clock, they assumed you were either ill or lazy.

By the time Lucas returned, freshly washed and dressed, I had two travel mugs of coffee and sandwiches ready. I had also learned sometimes it was a long way between fast-food restaurants in Amish Country.

"Let's go," I said.

Lucas nodded; his expression set with quiet determination.

CHAPTER 3

The first thing Lucas wanted to do was check the route Samuel always took while bicycling to his job at the sawmill.

"Perhaps he fell and hurt himself," Lucas said. "We need to make certain he's not lying somewhere, unable to get help. Turn right, please."

I turned right. As we drove along the country road, I noticed a buggy far ahead that seemed to weave erratically.

"That looks worrisome," I said, pointing.

Lucas frowned. "The driver might be inexperienced. Or the horse easily spooked."

We watched as a passing truck honked loudly, causing the horse to rear slightly before the buggy straightened out.

"That happens too often," Lucas said. "Not everyone slows down for buggies. I've had many close calls myself."

I slowed instinctively, the mere thought of Lucas in danger making me cautious. "Do the reflective triangles some Amish add to the back of their buggies help?"

"It's a little help, I suppose. Though some of the stricter orders still resist. They say if it's God's will for them to be hit…" He trailed off, his expression troubled.

"That is so sad!"

"It is the reality of our life," he said simply. "We accept these risks as part of our path."

After a thoughtful silence, we continued our search for Samuel. After we passed his sister's house, Lucas directed me to slow down to a crawl while he scanned both sides of the road all the way to the lumberyard. That wasn't difficult because there really wasn't anywhere along the way for a man to get lost. It was all flat farmland. No broken bike or injured man lying on either side of the road.

"Is there any other route he could have taken?"

"Not really." Lucas strained forward, as though he thought being a few more inches closer to the windshield would make it easier to scan the area. "Nothing that makes sense."

"Tell me more about your brother-in-law," I said. "I only met him that one time and we were all focused on the children and the pony,"

"There isn't a lot to tell." Lucas shrugged. "Samuel and I grew up together. When Gretchen married him, I was glad because I knew he would be good to her and good to their children. He's a hard worker and a loving father. There's not much more I can say about him. That's who he is—or at least who I thought he was."

"I'm guessing it's not normal for an Amish man to leave his family?"

"It is so rare I have never personally known someone to do it."

"Are you absolutely certain there were no marital problems?" I prodded. "I've been blindsided by the breakup of some of my friends. I thought they had marriages made in heaven, but I was wrong. And then there are my mother's five divorces."

He was silent, probably contemplating the strangeness of anyone having five divorces, but he chose not to comment on my mother. I think she scared him a little. Sometimes she scared me a little, too.

My mother, Desiree Stanton, is much admired for her beauty.

With the right makeup, she looks twenty-nine, pretends she's thirty-eight, and she insisted I ignore her forty-ninth birthday this year.

"Samuel always seemed at peace, so certain of our ways, content with his life." Lucas gazed out at the passing fields. "No one but God can truly know a man's heart, but I struggle to believe my brother-in-law would ever abandon his family."

"And you?" I asked. "Are you always so certain of your ways, content with your life?"

His eyes met mine briefly before returning to the road. "The bishop would say I think too much."

"Is that a bad thing?"

"It is neither good nor bad, it's just the way things are." Lucas adjusted his hat. "There are things about the *Englisch* world that I find useful. Knowledge. Ideas. Conveniences. But those comforts come with a price we Amish are not willing to pay, like the loss of community. The endless race for more." He smiled slightly. "Though I admit, during my *Rumspringa*, I was rather rebellious."

This statement was intriguing. No matter how hard I tried, I could not imagine Lucas ever being anything other than the hardworking Amish farmer I knew.

"So, what terrible things did you do as a teenager, Lucas?" I teased. "Let me guess. Did you rebel by wearing store-bought jeans? Getting a haircut? Growing a mustache? Or were you a really bad boy who went to wild barn parties and dated *Englisch* girls?"

"Nothing like that. Getting drunk and throwing up in someone's barn did not appeal to me and *Englisch* girls just made me nervous. But I got an *Englisch* haircut for a while, and I bought a pair of store-bought jeans and a dress shirt. And cowboy boots. I really loved those cowboy boots."

"I guess my biggest rebellion was books. There was so much I wanted to know. I got a library card and read books by the armload that my bishop would have forbidden had he known." He sounded amused at the admission. "And music. I liked classic rock, and I still miss listening to it. But I chose the Amish way because I believe it is best, not because I am ignorant of the alternatives."

Before I could respond, he pointed to a large white house on the right. "Please turn in here. This belongs to one of Samuel's brothers."

I waited in the car as Lucas knocked on Samuel's brother's door. It opened. He went inside, stayed a few minutes, then came out, holding a loaf of something wrapped in a dish towel, and climbed inside the car.

"No luck?" I asked.

"Adam has not seen or heard from him." He held up the loaf. "His oldest girl was baking banana nut bread. She sent a loaf home with me."

"Of course she did," I said, with a hint of a smile. I had already discovered that the Amish were generous with their baked goods. "Where to next?"

"His brother, Virgil, lives one mile further. He owns a furniture shop and ships his pieces all over the country. He works through a website run by *Englisch* people,"

"That sounds rather progressive."

"Virgil walks the line," Lucas explained. "He doesn't use the computer himself, but he's not opposed to hiring others who do. The bishop allows it because Virgil employs eight families from our community."

I drove another mile to Virgil's place, another well-maintained white farmhouse with a large workshop visible behind it. Again, I waited in the car.

After seeing Lucas disappear into the workshop. I'd barely gotten my laptop open before he returned to the car.

"Nothing?" I asked as he got back inside.

"Virgil hasn't seen Samuel since church last Sunday."

I started the car again.

"Take a left out of the driveway," Lucas said. "I want to go see

Samuel's mother and father, and then we'll go see Matthew. He lives two miles north of here."

"How many brothers does Samuel have?" I turned left.

"Eleven," Lucas said absently, as though that was the most natural thing in the world.

"And how many sisters?"

Lucas was silent for a moment, thinking. "Five."

I did a quick calculation. "His mother and father had seventeen children?"

"Yes. Samuel is the youngest."

"Isn't that a little excessive?"

"Children are a blessing from the Lord," Lucas said.

Easy for you to say, I thought, wondering how Samuel's mother felt. I was surprised the woman was still alive after having that many children.

At the next house where we stopped, a tall Amish woman rose effortlessly from where she had been kneeling beside a rock-bordered flower garden. The bottom of her green dress was stained with dirt, and tendrils of blonde hair had come loose from her choring kerchief. As she rose, she wiped the sweat from her face with the back of her hand, leaving an accidental smudge of earth across her forehead.

She picked up a plastic ice cream bucket, and walked toward us with long, unhurried strides that gave her an elegance I envied.

"Is that one of Samuel's sisters?" I asked.

"No," Lucas said. "That's his mother."

"It isn't possible," I said under my breath.

"What? Did you think a woman who had birthed seventeen children wouldn't be able to still walk?" He chuckled as he opened the car door. "It may not be possible, but that is Samuel's mother."

As she drew closer, I saw she was older than I'd realized. Her blonde hair had threads of gray, and her face was etched with fine lines.

"Any *wort* from *mei sohn?*" She sat the bucket on the ground and wiped her hands on her apron. "Gretchen told me she was going to *komm* get you."

"*Nee*, nothing yet," Lucas said. "I was hoping you'd heard something from him by now."

"Not a *wort*. Been praying about it *alle* morning while I worked on my *blumen*. It is *recht* late to be thinning them, but Earnest has *net* been so *gut*."

"I heard. How is he doing?" Lucas asked.

"Today is not so much pain. A *gut* day. But tomorrow, who knows?" She shrugged. "*Gott's wille sei getan.*"

"Yes, God's will be done," Lucas echoed. "I will pray for more good days."

"*Danki.*" She bent down and glanced into the car at me. "Do you like irises?" she asked hopefully.

Her face was weathered but calm, and I couldn't look away. This woman had raised seventeen children, and was presently watching her husband slip from this world, and still—*still*—she found time to kneel beside her garden and tend to beauty.

The sun caught the silver threads in her hair as she looked at me, her expression deeply kind. There was something holy in it—not the kind that preaches, but the kind that stays, and plants things.

"I do love irises." It wasn't entirely a lie. I wasn't certain what an iris looked like, but I knew it was a flower, and I liked flowers.

"Here, take *diese*." She handed me the ice cream bucket through the window. It was filled with flower bulbs and dirt. I handed it to Lucas as soon as he got buckled in.

I had zero experience planting flower bulbs. I wasn't sure if she had given me a gift, or a chore, and I didn't care.

She must have seen the uncertainty in my face. "Just stick them in the *erde*. They will grow."

"Thank you for the flower bulbs," I called out the window as we drove away. She didn't smile or wave. She just gave a quick nod, watching us leave.

"I'd like to know her better." I rolled up the window.

"You would have to be prepared to work alongside her while you did," Lucas said. "I don't think I've ever seen her sit down for more than a minute. She's not one to chat. That's the longest conversation I've ever had with her, and I grew up here."

Something was bothering me. "Why isn't her eleven sons and five daughters out searching for Samuel? Why is it your job?"

Lucas was silent for several beats. Lucas thought things out before he talked. It had been difficult to get used to, but I had learned to expect it.

"I suppose in a family of seventeen, people learn not to get easily upset over things," Lucas said. "Samuel's brothers probably figure he had his reasons for leaving and will come home when he's ready."

"Do you think he'll come back?"

"If he can," Lucas said. "But I'm wondering if there might be something Gretchen is too embarrassed to tell me."

"Like what?"

"Samuel borrowed money from Virgil last week. He said that he and Gretchen were running short this month and needed a little help."

"That doesn't sound good."

"No, and it doesn't sound like Gretchen. Even as a little girl, she was always good at pinching a penny. Samuel makes a decent salary at the mill and is content for her to take care of the family finances because she's so good at it."

"Then maybe Samuel needed money, and he didn't want Gretchen to know," I said.

"That's what I'm thinking," Lucas said.

The hidden loan could be our first real clue to Samuel's disappearance.

CHAPTER 4

LUCAS

Lucas rarely hired drivers, but when he did, he spent as little time talking with them as possible. Being around the *Englisch* too long could become worrisome. For instance, he never knew when they would begin asking questions about his religion. The questions ranged from innocently ignorant to downright rude.

Often, he had no good answers, anyway. Why did one Amish sect allow battery-powered tools, and another sect only allow hand tools? Why did one sect allow windshields on their buggies, and another sect forbid them?

How should he know? He wasn't a bishop. Different bishops allowed different things. That's the only reason he could give. That and the one the Amish gave to one another, that a certain rule just was and always had been.

There were some major benefits to being Amish—the strong network of friends and family was one—but the convoluted ways the forty-something different Amish sects chose to live their lives were as much a mystery to him as they were to the *Englisch* standing on the outside looking in.

When he finally committed to baptism and fully joined the church, it wasn't because his questions had been answered. It was because he'd decided that community and tradition were worth the sacrifice of certain freedoms. Yet even now, years later, he occasionally found himself drawn to the complex world beyond his community. This is why being around the *Englisch*, except for short periods of time for business purposes—made him nervous.

That was true for Amy Stanton as well. If he'd realized how restless he would feel sitting in a car with her while she drove him all over the countryside, he never would have asked. He would have called one of several *Englisch* drivers who lived nearby instead.

There was nothing wrong with Amy to cause such restlessness. The problem was there was too much that was right with her.

He was lonely after three long years as a widower. If Amy was Amish, he would seriously consider courting her. But if Amy had been raised Amish, she wouldn't be who she was—and that was the problem. Was he attracted to her merely because she was different from anything he'd ever known?

His father would have cautioned him. "Better to marry a plain woman with a good heart than a pretty one who turns your head from God's ways," he'd often said. But Amy possessed a depth that reminded him of the best Amish women he knew, yet with a worldliness that both intrigued and unsettled him.

Whatever it was, he realized that spending too much time this close to her, encapsulated in this car, was not wise. She smelled good, and she glanced over at him too often with that pretty smile. He even admired how expertly she handled her car.

"Turn here," he instructed as they came upon the private road that led to the sawmill where Samuel worked.

"I thought your sister had already gone to the mill early this morning, and no one had seen him."

"She did."

Amy asked no follow up question. She just turned onto the road. As they approached the mill, he felt like he owed her an explanation.

"I'm certain the men were telling the truth when they told her that Samuel had not come into work yesterday, but Gretchen is his wife. They might know something else they didn't feel right about telling her, but they might tell me."

"That's smart," Amy said. "It's the old boys' club mentality. If they suspect another woman is involved, for instance, they might tell you, but never his wife—especially with Samuel's three little daughters standing beside her."

"Something like that," Lucas said. "This might take a while. Are you okay with staying in the car?"

"Take your time."

As Lucas walked toward the mill, he couldn't help but wish that Rick had bequeathed his farm and all his possessions to a male relative instead of this lovely young woman.

The sawmill's familiar scent of fresh-cut lumber and machine oil greeted him as he entered. He said a quick prayer as he stepped into the noisy building, asking for wisdom and clarity about his good friend Samuel—and for strength to keep his heart properly guarded around Amy Stanton.

CHAPTER 5

I got two pages written while Lucas was in the sawmill questioning Samuel's co-workers. He stayed about forty-five minutes, which was just long enough to worry me.

When he came out, he was frowning, and there was sawdust on his hat and beard. He stopped to brush it off before he stepped in.

I tucked my laptop behind the seat and started the car. "What did you find out?"

"Samuel had a visitor a few days before he disappeared."

My heart sank. I knew what was coming next—or I thought I did.

"A woman?"

"Yes, an *Englisch* woman."

"Attractive?"

"They said she was very attractive, but she looked old enough to be his mother. One of them remembered she introduced herself as a doctor, but no one remembered her actual name except it sounded foreign."

"A doctor?" I mulled this over. "Then what happened?"

"Samuel walked outside with her. They talked for a few minutes.

When he came back inside, he was wiping away tears. They said Samuel wouldn't talk about it and was quiet for the rest of the day."

"What do you think that meant?" I asked.

"I don't know," Lucas said. "Except that either he is sick and not telling anyone about it, or perhaps I did not know my brother-in-law as well as I thought I did."

"Did they notice any change in his behavior in the days after that?"

"They said he was distracted. One man said he overheard Samuel talking about hospital procedures with another worker who used to be an EMT. When the coworker asked why he was interested, Samuel just said he was curious."

I considered this new information as we continued our search. A mysterious, older, doctor, Samuel's emotional reaction, and a sudden interest in hospitals. It didn't sound good.

"Do you think there's a chance he's really sick and doesn't want Gretchen to know?"

"I've never known a doctor with the time to drive to people's workplaces to tell them they're sick," Lucas said. "If something is wrong with him, Gretchen would know, and she would tell me so I could at least pray for him."

I lost track of the houses we stopped at that day. After a while, they became a blur. Lucas didn't stay for long at any of them. Often, he came away with a small gift. A jar of jam. Some maple syrup. A container of honey. A fresh cherry pie. By the time we got home, we were both exhausted and disappointed. We were no closer to finding Samuel, but we were well-provisioned.

"Well," I said. "That was an interesting trip."

"At least we know many places not to look or inquire."

"Are you sure it wouldn't be a good idea to contact the police?" I asked.

"And what do you think they will do?" Lucas said, tiredly. "Unless I am mistaken, runaway fathers and husbands are not uncommon in your world. I doubt they would spend much energy on an Amish man who has broken no law and has been missing less than forty-eight hours. They might think he'd just wanted to go fishing."

"True." Still, I couldn't let go of the idea that maybe Samuel wasn't as wonderful as Lucas thought. "If you had a wife and children, what could make you leave them?"

With quiet, intense passion, he said, "If the Lord blessed me with a wife and children, there is nothing on earth that could make me leave them."

My heart skipped a beat. Any Amish woman who might be lucky enough to get Lucas as a husband would be one fortunate woman indeed.

When we got home, Lucas unloaded our unexpected haul of flower bulbs and edibles into my kitchen, then went to the barn to catch up on some chores. I couldn't think of anything more to do now except get some more words written while I could. Concentrating on my writing was a lot easier with Lucas gone.

I remembered an old TV commercial quoting a rule of physics about a body in motion staying in motion, and a body at rest, staying at rest. They used it to sell running shoes, and it was a good ad. Six years later, I still have the running shoes I bought because of that commercial. They're still brand new.

That rule is never truer than in the work of a writer. Once I'm really into a story, there is an impetus that begins and grows to where I'll sometimes find myself typing faster and faster because the ideas and words just keep pouring out. Sometimes, when that happens, I type with my eyes closed because it's like my mind is creating a movie and it's all I can do to keep up with describing what my mind is seeing.

Unfortunately, this was not one of those times. I sat at the computer and forced myself to put words on the page, hoping to prime the pump, so to speak. All I managed to produce were random words, a couple of incomplete sentences, and a stab at writing a paragraph that was so boring I deleted it.

This was a shame because the story I had been hired to write had wonderful potential. A family had entrusted me with the letters, diaries, and an unfinished memoir chronicling the life of their mother, a woman who was a military nurse during World War II.

She'd been stationed in the Philippines when our bases were attacked by the Japanese the day after they bombed Pearl Harbor. She and seventy-six other military nurses were captured and spent three years as POWs. Despite starvation rations, those nurses continued to care for the sick and wounded. They were referred to by our soldiers as The Angels of Bataan.

It was a life well worth writing about. It had everything people love in a story. Exotic destinations, danger, romance, and heroism in the face of evil.

But even with such a riveting story to work on, it was in the past. Samuel's disappearance was happening in the present. The only thing I could think about were those three little Amish girls and their worried mother. I felt like I should do something, but I couldn't figure out what.

I'm fairly certain Lucas was struggling with the same thoughts.

I stared at the blank screen and tried to think of something more we could do. I knew from television shows how important the first few hours were after a disappearance. It felt wrong just to sit here going about my usual business.

About that time, someone knocked on my back door. I didn't have time to go open it before my nearest Amish neighbor, Erma, stuck her head in. She was wearing her choring scarf instead of her *kapp*, so I knew she'd been in a hurry to get here. This wasn't just a social visit.

Erma's quick knock was more of a "Hello, I'm coming in" than a request to enter. That was something else I was getting used to. Neighbors and friends didn't always wait politely for someone to come to the door. There was an unspoken rule that front doors were for salespeople and strangers. Those people were expected to knock and wait. Back doors were for friends and neighbors to have the freedom to come and go. I'd given up keeping my door locked except at night.

All the years I'd lived in New York City, I'd never questioned the need to keep multiple locks on my door, so this open-door policy had been a challenge for me.

"Hey, Erma." Lucas came in from the barn. He took off his work boots before stepping into the kitchen.

"Adam's wife just stopped by and told me about Samuel," she said. "I came as soon as I heard. Is there anything I can do?"

"I'm not sure," Lucas said. "I'm still trying to figure things out."

"Do you mind telling me what you know?" Erma asked. "I want to help."

"I'll make coffee while Lucas fills you in," I said.

"Some of that banana bread might taste good," Lucas said as he slid into one of the sturdy oak chairs.

He seemed comfortable in my kitchen. I knew he'd spent many hours here talking with Rick, my ex-stepfather, over the years. His long legs looked good, stretched out beneath my kitchen table. I even liked the looks of his stocking feet. One of his sisters made extra money knitting homemade socks, and he had bought several pairs from her.

I filled a coffee pot and sat it on the stove. Rick had used an old-fashioned percolator, and I'd grown to like the stronger flavor.

While I sliced the banana bread, Lucas filled Erma in on the details.

"Something bad has happened to him," Erma said firmly, after Lucas had finished. "Amish men with pregnant wives and small children do not run away from their responsibilities."

"Gretchen is pregnant?" I asked, surprised.

"Five months," Lucas said.

"How come Erma knew, and I didn't?"

"Church," Erma answered. "The meal we have afterward serves the same purpose as your people's social media—but without the pictures. I've known about Gretchen's new baby for the past three months."

I liked Erma, I really did, but this comment annoyed me. I couldn't help it if I didn't go to her Amish church. It wasn't as though anyone had ever invited me. I was also getting a little tired of hearing the praises of Amish men. "Sometimes people have moments of weakness, regardless of their religious beliefs. I bet some Amish man somewhere has broken ranks and fled the responsibilities of supporting a wife and child."

"No doubt," Erma said. "But not Samuel. I don't think I've ever known anyone with a more giving heart."

Erma went on and on for a while about all of Samuel's wonderful traits. A loving father, a devoted husband, and a considerate and dedicated church member who was ready to help anyone at any time.

A suspicion crossed my mind. "Is Samuel any relation to you?"

"He's my oldest sister's boy." Erma helped herself to a second slice of banana bread. "I used to babysit him back when she worked with her husband in their buggy shop. He was the sweetest child. Never knew him to do anything wrong. Men like Samuel don't go wandering off."

"Perhaps it's time to go to the police now," I said.

"We rarely go to the police." Erma became instantly defensive.

"Why not?" I asked. Even though Lucas had already said no to the idea, I wanted to hear what Erma would say.

The coffee had finally finished percolating. I poured a cup for each of us and sat out a small pitcher of cream.

"It's hard for outsiders to understand our culture." Erma poured a dollop of cream into her coffee. "When things go wrong, it just seems to work out better if we take care of our own problems."

"Except for Rachel," Lucas said. "I've been thinking it might be wise to talk to her."

"Who is Rachel?" I asked.

"Rachel Troyer is a Sugarcreek cop," Lucas answered. "She was raised by her three Old Order Amish aunts after her parents died. When she grew up, she chose not to become Amish, but she speaks our language and knows our ways. She will understand why we are so concerned."

"I heard she left the police force," Erma said.

"Is it because of the new baby?" Lucas asked.

"Yes, but she's also helping her husband out with that new restaurant he and his brother started."

As they shared information, I marveled at the knowledge of the local people they shared. When I'd been in my apartment in New York City, I'd had no idea who lived in the adjoining apartment.

"I would not mind going to talk to her," Lucas said. "We were in the same grade in school."

"A woman cop went to an Amish school?" I asked.

"Rachel was one of us for most of her young life," Lucas said. "I would trust any advice she might give."

"Then, let's go see her!" I was already reaching for my car keys. The thought of finally taking action—any action—lifted my spirits.

"I'll tidy up," Erma said. "Tell Rachel hello for me."

CHAPTER 6

It was dark by the time we got to Joe's Home Plate. The restaurant was filled with baseball memorabilia—signed jerseys in glass frames, weathered gloves mounted on wooden plaques, and vintage team photos covering nearly every inch of wall space. Apparently, Rachel's husband, Joe, had been a big deal in the sport for a while.

A woman Lucas identified as Rachel stood behind the cash register as she finished ringing up a customer. She had light brown hair pulled into a ponytail and over her jeans and t-shirt she wore a gray stretchy wrap around her middle which held a baby. Its little face looked out at the world with sleepy eyes while cuddled safely against its mother's heart.

"Hey there Lucas." Rachel spotted him as soon as we walked in. "How are you?"

"I am well," Lucas said. "I see you have a beautiful new *boppli*."

"I do!" Rachel's smile was huge. "Joe and I have a son and a daughter now. How blessed can one woman be, right?"

"I am happy for you, Rachel," Lucas said. "Do you have a few minutes?"

"Of course." Rachel motioned for one of the servers to take over her place at the register. Then she led us to an empty table.

"This is Amy Stanton." Lucas introduced me as we sat down. "Rick Downey's stepdaughter. She's the one who inherited his farm."

"Welcome to Sugarcreek," Rachel said. "I've heard about you. My Amish aunts were divided in their opinions of whether you would stay or go back to New York City."

That puzzled me. "Why would your aunts care?"

"Have you ever noticed that many women become addicted to soap operas later in life? Being Amish, my aunts don't have television, so the people around them become one big daytime TV drama. When you first moved here, they must have spent at least two days debating the merits of living in New York City versus staying in Sugarcreek and wondering which you would choose to do."

"How would they even know about it?" I asked.

"The man who delivers your mail is their first cousin. He kept them informed."

I felt a little uncomfortable with the idea that complete strangers had been discussing my life in that much detail.

"Never underestimate the Amish grapevine," Rachel said.

The baby began to fuss. Rachel stood up and started to sway and bounce until the little thing settled down again. She resumed her seat but remained perched on the edge. "What's wrong, Lucas?"

Lucas told her about Samuel's disappearance, his voice low and steady but unable to hide his concern. As he spoke, I gazed at the baby's sweet little nose and face. Babies were so nice. I wondered what it would be like to have one of my own someday. In New York, I'd been focused entirely on my career. Here in Sugarcreek, surrounded by so many families, I was noticing a stirring of different desires of someday having a family of my own.

"So, let me repeat what you just told me from a cop's perspective," Rachel said, drawing me back to the conversation. "Samuel has committed no crime. He has no criminal record. He's a healthy young man with no impairments. The only issue is that his wife is complaining that he left yesterday morning and didn't return."

"Yes."

"Few cops would take this seriously. At least not until he's gone a few more days. They would look at the fact that he had three small children, a pregnant wife, a physically demanding job, and they would assume he'd gotten fed up and took a hike, probably straight to a new girlfriend's house. It happens all the time."

"I know," Lucas said. "But…"

"But we're talking about your brother-in-law, Samuel," Rachel said. "Whom I've known since grade school. That makes it a whole other issue, doesn't it? Samuel was an honorable man who would cut off his arm before he would abandon Gretchen and those little girls. If he hasn't been seen in the past two days, there is a definite reason for concern."

"I thought so."

There was relief in Lucas's voice. Rachel was not downplaying his concern or giving empty assurances. She was giving his concern the attention it deserved.

"You've already talked to everyone who might have seen him?"

"Everyone I could think of."

"You've looked in every ditch and field between his home and workplace for any sign of him?"

"Only briefly from the car. Not on foot," Lucas said.

"I don't suppose you have a photo of him?" Rachel asked.

I reached into my purse for my phone. I had a recent photo of Samuel. I'd taken it when they'd brought the girls over to the farm to see their new pony.

"No. He and my sister are quite strict about the church's no picture rule."

I took my hand out of my purse. What was I supposed to do? Ignore the fact that I had a perfectly good, clear photo of Samuel holding little Laura?

"And he doesn't use credit cards?" Rachel asked.

"Gretchen is fearful of getting into debt, so they own no credit or debit cards."

I was in a quandary. Should I confess I had taken a forbidden photo of Samuel? I had taken it soon after I moved to Sugarcreek, before I knew there was a rule against it.

"What kind of transportation did he use that morning?"

I reached into my purse again and quietly brought out my phone.

"His bicycle." Lucas said. "No one has seen it. It isn't at his workplace or at his home. I checked."

Rachel nodded, thinking. "I will pass this information on to the police chief, along with my concern and opinion of the gravity of the situation. He and the deputies will be on the alert for any clues about Samuel's whereabouts—but other than what's already been done, with nothing to trace and no photo to show around, I don't know what else we can do for now."

I'd been growing more and more uncomfortable as they talked. I knew I needed to say something, even if it was embarrassing to do so, but how would Lucas react? Would he be angry? Disappointed in me? How important was the no photos rule to him? Then I thought about Gretchen's little girls and my resistance melted. If there was the slightest chance that the photo could help us find Samuel, Lucas's disappointment in me would be a small price to pay.

I'd been scrolling through my cell phone photo gallery for the past few seconds and had found what I was looking for.

"Maybe you could use this." I handed my cell phone to Rachel.

Rachel looked down at my phone, then back up at me with surprise. "This is an excellent photo. When did you take it?"

"A few weeks ago. Samuel and Gretchen and the girls came to the farm to get a pony."

"Why did you photograph my brother-in-law?" Lucas asked, perplexed. I was grateful that I'd had time to come up with a plausible answer.

"Little Laura was in her daddy's arms, and she looked so cute sitting there in her bonnet. I couldn't help myself."

I didn't mention the fact that Lucas was standing beside his brother-in-law that day, and it was such a handsome shot of him I'd felt compelled to take the picture. However, while he and Rachel were talking, I'd cropped him out, so Samuel and Laura were the only ones visible.

"I often wish you *Englisch* did not find us so photogenic." Lucas sighed. "But now, I am grateful. May I see it?"

Rachel handed it to him. The close-up of father and daughter—both with matching blue eyes—was quite arresting.

"Do you think it will help?" I asked.

"It certainly won't hurt," Rachel said. "Unofficially, the first thing I'd advise you to do is get some of your people together and walk the route he took every day. Watch for anything. There aren't a lot of houses along that stretch of road, but at the ones that are, show the inhabitants the photo of your brother-in-law and ask if they saw him. Look for his bicycle. Finding it might be key."

The baby was starting to fuss again, so Rachel stood up again and began to sway and pat the baby's bottom. "Did Gretchen see him leave? Is she sure he was headed toward the mill?"

"She didn't see him leave," Lucas said.

"This whole thing is so odd," Rachel said. "Amish men like Samuel don't just disappear. Let me know if you find out anything. In the meantime, I think your best hope is this photo. Make lots of copies. Scatter them around and then pray that someone knows something or saw something.

"*Danki*," Lucas said. "You are a good friend, Rachel."

As we left the restaurant, I noticed him standing a little straighter, his steps more purposeful. Having a plan, however modest, seemed to have lifted some of the weight from his shoulders.

When we got home, I designed an eight-and-a-half by eleven-inch flyer using Samuel's photo. Lucas began contacting people from church. The next day was going to be one of their no-church Sundays. Taking a walk was a common activity for Amish people on their no-church Sunday when the weather was nice. Lucas put out the word for everyone to meet at Gretchen's house at eight o'clock in the morning so the sun would be fully up.

As I watched the copies emerge from my printer, I felt a growing sense that I was becoming more invested in this community than I'd ever intended to be, but grateful I was being given a chance to become part of it. Lucas gathered the stack of flyers. "I'll take these to Gretchen's and let her know what we've done and what we're planning to do tomorrow."

"Do you want me to come with you?" I asked.

He considered it briefly, then shook his head. "It's getting late. She'll be putting the girls to bed. Besides, you've already done more than enough today."

After he left, I sat down at my computer to get some work done, but my brain was too tired to concentrate. All I could do was delete a few emails. Tomorrow would be another day of searching, and I needed to be rested. I went to bed early, ready to get up and walk with Lucas's people to see if we could find anything.

CHAPTER 7

LUCAS

Lucas's niece, Sarah, was standing on her tiptoes, pegging laundry on the clothesline in their backyard, when Lucas arrived at Gretchen's house. Ruth was handing her the washcloths, and Laura was holding the bag of clothespins. Sarah reached out her hand, and Laura placed a clothes pin in it.

This was disturbing. The girls were doing a good job, but it was five o'clock in the afternoon. Gretchen never hung out her laundry later than eight o'clock in the morning, usually on Monday and, if necessary, on Fridays or Saturdays.

When they caught sight of him, they dropped their tasks and ran to him. "*Onkel* Lucas!" they called out in delight. He caught all three in his arms and lifted them up in a hug. They were as precious to him as if they were his own.

"Have you found *Daett?*" Sarah asked.

"*Nee,*" he admitted. "But I have gone to many places where he is not."

"This is not *gut,*" Sarah said, her small face solemn.

"It isn't," he said. "Where is your *mamm?*"

"Lying down," Sarah said. "She isn't feeling *gut.*"

47

Ruth nodded solemnly and placed her hands over her little belly, as though in sympathy.

"The midwife was here and said that *Mamm* has to stay in bed until the pains go away."

"How long has this been going on?"

"Since this morning. She got our laundry washed, but when she started to hang everything up, the pains started."

"She's only five months along with the *boppli*," Lucas said, worry creasing his brow.

"The midwife is upset," Sarah said. "She thinks this wouldn't have happened if *Daett* hadn't left."

"Did she say that to you?" Lucas was appalled. The midwife was *Englisch*, but certainly she knew better than to criticize the girls' father in front of them.

"*Nee*, I heard her talking to the doctor on her pocket phone," Sarah said. "She didn't know I heard her."

"I'm going inside to talk to your *mamm*," he said. "You *kinner* stay here in the yard."

"*Yah*, we will," Sarah said. "There's still a lot of work to be done."

When Lucas entered his sister's bedroom, he was struck by how quietly she lay in the bed. He had seldom seen Gretchen so motionless.

"*Bischt du awwright?*" He pulled up a ladderback chair and sat down next to her.

"I'm afraid to move for fear the cramps will start back up again," she said.

"You should not be alone right now," he said. "I will come stay with you and the *kinner*."

"You are a *gut bruder*, but that isn't necessary. Samuel's *mamm* and his youngest *schweschder* are coming to help. I will be in good hands." She took hold of his arm. "But tell me, what of Samuel? Have you a word?"

In her condition, Lucas didn't want to mention the older woman who had come to see Samuel at the sawmill, but there was one thing he needed to ask. "Were you and Samuel having financial troubles?"

"*Gewiss net.* You know how careful I am with *geld.* Why would you ask such a thing?"

"Because he went to his brother Virgil, asking for a loan for five hundred dollars."

"Did Virgil give it to him?"

"Yes."

"I don't know why Samuel would do such a thing. We have nearly twenty-thousand dollars in the bank, Lucas." Her voice grew plaintive. "I don't understand."

"Neither do I," Lucas said. "But I'm trying to find out. I went to Rachel Troyer today. She asked if we had a picture to show around."

"I don't."

"I know, but Amy did." He took the paper with Samuel's photo on it from inside his jacket and handed it to her.

She gazed at the photo of Samuel with Laura in his arms. Then she traced his face with her fingers. "It is a *gut* likeness, but why was Amy taking pictures of my husband?"

"She's *Englisch.*" He shrugged. "That's what they do."

"And this time, I am grateful. May I keep this?"

"*Gviss.* We made many copies on her printer. Rachel said to show them to people who live between here and the sawmill and ask if they've seen him."

Gretchen took the paper with the photo on it and pressed it to her heart. "He is a *gut* man, Lucas."

"I have always thought so."

"He would not deliberately abandon me and the *kinner.*"

"Of course, he wouldn't." He busied himself straightening the covers.

"He was hoping for a *bu* this time."

"If you have a boy, the girls will make a pet of him."

She smiled at that. "They would."

"I must ask you one more thing," he said. "And remember—I am your *bruder*. You can tell me and I will keep it to myself, but I must know… were you and Samuel having any trouble?"

"You mean arguments?"

"Yes."

"That's the thing," she said. "We never did. Ever. He was so kind to me, and I was kind to him back. We were happy. There was much love in this *Haus*. There was no reason for him to run away from our home. That is what makes me so afraid for him. I don't think my husband would leave us unless someone forced him to."

Lucas took her hand between both of his. "*Mir bete*," he said softly. "We will pray, and we will find him."

A tear slipped down Gretchen's cheek. "*Danki*, Lucas," she whispered. "You are truly a blessing."

CHAPTER 8

I got up before dawn on Sunday morning, ready to walk the route along with the people from Lucas's church.

This had brought out approximately sixty Amish men and women willing to walk the route and question neighbors. By noon, they had turned up nothing. Lucas thanked them for their help.

"*Denki for eier hilf,*" he said with genuine appreciation—and told them to go back home. A few of the women stayed behind to spend time with Gretchen, because that was the Amish way. When trouble came to an Amish door, so did help.

However, the search for Samuel caused word of his disappearance to spread from house to house and the full weight of the Amish grapevine was brought to bear on the fact that this young father had come up missing. Letters were written. Some Amish teenagers on *Rumspringa* turned to social media, as did several ex-Amish who knew of or were related to Gretchen and Samuel's families.

By Monday, copies of the picture I'd taken were all nailed to various telephone and electric posts around the county—carried by Amish men and women on horses and bicycles.

On Tuesday, an article was published on the front page of The

Budget, the Sugarcreek newspaper, along with the picture of Samuel. It was then that the national news picked up on the story. Somehow a missing Amish father was a bigger story than a missing *Englisch* father. I was told later that reported sightings of Samuel began pouring into the Sugarcreek police station from as far away as Quebec.

Most of the calls involved genuinely concerned people reporting they had seen an Amish man resembling Samuel on a bicycle. This became an issue because what with having virtually the same hat, clothes, beard, and haircut, there was a sameness about all Amish men of about Samuel's age that made it hard for *Englisch* people to discern one specific Amish man from another. The photograph really wasn't that much help, especially in the *Englisch* community.

On Wednesday, a break came. The journalist who had written the article for The Budget contacted the sheriff about a call received by the newspaper. Someone who worked at the New Philadelphia Greyhound bus station had seen the article and remembered that a plastic grocery bag of what appeared to be Amish clothing had been left behind in the men's bathroom.

The custodian had put the grocery bag of clothing away in case someone came to claim it. The sheriff called Rachel, who went to collect it. She then called me to bring Lucas to the station to see if he could positively identify it as Samuel's.

He couldn't. There is a sameness to Amish men's clothing. To a man like Lucas, unacquainted with stitching and fabric, it could have been anyone's.

"We need to show it to Gretchen," Lucas said, his face drawn with concern. "She's the one who made all his clothing and washed and ironed them weekly."

"Then we'd better go pick up Gretchen," I said.

Gretchen was no longer in bed when we arrived. She met us at the door and invited us in with a quiet "*Kumm.*"

"How are you feeling?" Lucas asked.

"The cramps stopped," she answered. "And I have too much work to do to stay in bed."

Her stoicism slipped into puzzlement when Lucas explained she needed to go with us to the Sugarcreek police station to identify some clothing that might be Samuel's.

"Samuel's *glaeder?*" she said. "Why would he leave his clothes behind?"

"They might not even be his," Lucas said. "Maybe some Amish teenager discarded them before leaving for a *Rumspringa* trip. We just need to make sure that they aren't Samuel's."

One of Samuel's sisters stayed with the three children while we drove the short distance to the police station.

Officer Rachel Troyer was already there. After a few words of greeting, she pulled on latex gloves and began taking the clothing out of the bag one item at a time.

"Does anything look familiar?" she asked.

"This is my Samuel's coat." Gretchen pointed to a group of stitches on the elbow. "He snagged it on a barbed wire fence. It was the day after Laura was born. He said he didn't want to give me another task on top of childbirth, so he got a needle and thread and mended it himself. He was not very skilled, but it held."

"What about this?" A young male officer wheeled a bicycle into the station. "Does this look like your husband's bike?"

"That's Samuel's," Gretchen said, her voice barely above a whisper. "He's had it since before we married. Where was it?"

"I found it behind the New Philadelphia bus station. It looks like he went to some trouble to hide it beneath some brush."

"That makes no sense. Why would Samuel hide his bicycle and throw away his Amish clothing?" Gretchen said, shaking her head.

Except for Gretchen, I'm pretty certain we were all thinking the same thing. Samuel had selfishly run away from his responsibilities. He had abandoned his pregnant wife and his three little daughters.

I was grateful, and I'm certain Gretchen and Lucas were also, that the three girls weren't there. Gretchen would have at least a little time to absorb this latest news before she went home to them. I knew Sarah would be filled with questions to which her mother would have no easy answers.

"I talked to the Greyhound station manager," Rachel said. "It's a busy place. The manager does not know what bus Samuel might have taken. Does he have any relatives or friends he might have visited, Gretchen?"

"All of his *brieder* un *schweschdere* live near here. Our friends live here. There is no one I can think of that he would go see," Gretchen said. She winced and gently rubbed her abdomen. "I would like to go back home to my children now, please."

Lucas placed a supportive hand on his sister's shoulder. "Of course," he said gently. "Let's take you home."

As they walked ahead of me toward the car, I noticed the way Gretchen leaned slightly against her brother's strength. Even in their grief and confusion, there was something beautiful about the way they supported one another. This was the Amish way—family standing together through any trial, no matter how bewildering.

CHAPTER 9

"Would you mind telling me what you're thinking?" Lucas and I had taken Gretchen home, helped her into bed, and left her in the competent care of her sister-in-law. Now, I was driving us home.

"I am thinking that Samuel is not right in the head," Lucas said. "He has everything a man could want. A loving wife. Three precious children. A new baby on the way. No debt. A decent amount of money tucked away for emergencies. How could any man walk away from all that? I can make no sense of it."

"I feel so sorry for Gretchen!"

"My sister is a grown woman, and she is not weak." Lucas sounded angry. "She will survive this."

I wanted to believe him, but his words seemed hollow given the circumstances. As if reading my thoughts, Lucas added, "You didn't see her after the fire."

"Fire?"

"Three years ago, lightning struck their barn. Everything was lost —the horses, the equipment, even Samuel's workshop. The entire community gathered to rebuild it, of course, but those first days…" He shook his head. "Samuel was in bed with pneumonia. Gretchen managed everything, temporary housing for the surviving animals, ordering building materials for the barn raising, and negotiations with the *Englisch* construction company that would provide the metal roof. She was eight months pregnant with Laura."

I pulled into my driveway, put the car in park, and turned toward Lucas to listen to the rest of his story.

"When I stopped by the day after the fire, I found her at the kitchen table, writing numbers in a ledger. Ruth was sound asleep in her lap, and Sarah was drawing pictures with crayons. Outside, there was a long line of freshly washed laundry drying in the sun. When I asked Gretchen how she was doing, she didn't answer me with a list of worries. Instead, she quoted one of our mother's favorite sayings, 'The Lord gives us strength for today's troubles, not tomorrow's.'"

His gaze was distant, remembering. "That's why I'm not as worried about Gretchen as I am about those little girls. My sister has always found her way through difficult times, but her three children break my heart. Daughters need a father to guide and protect them. Samuel knows that."

Lucas's statement brought a lump to my throat. I felt pity for Samuel's daughters, but I also felt a stab of sorrow for the little child I once was. What would it have been like to have had a father to guide and protect me, instead of dealing with a series of Mom's boyfriends and husbands?

I've never known who my father is.

My mother won't tell me. She's been married five times. She left her first husband, my father, before I was even born. My favorite ex-stepfather, Rick Downey, the one who left this farm and an antique store to me six months ago, was the closest thing to a father I ever had, but she divorced him when I was twelve.

I try not to dwell on it. Sometimes I make lighthearted jokes about it if someone asks too many questions, but it is always there in the back of my mind, and frankly, it hurts.

I tried to pry it out of her when I was younger, but she got defensive each time I asked, so eventually I stopped asking and tried to take it for granted that other little girls had dads, but I did not.

"I was raised without a father," I told Lucas.. "And I turned out okay."

"You father is missing?"

"Missing?" I gave a short laugh. "I guess you could call it that. I've never met him. My mom won't even tell me his name."

"You do not know your father's name?"

"I don't even know if he's alive."

"That is strange," Lucas said. "Even for the *Englisch*."

"I'm sure it does sound strange to you." I sounded a little bitter, but I didn't care. "Especially since you and your people can practically trace your ancestors back to the beginning of time."

"Not the beginning of time," Lucas corrected. "But a few hundred years, yes. Do you know what might have caused your mother to keep this from you?"

"No," I said. "When Desiree decides not to talk about something, she doesn't talk about it."

"You should ask again," he said. "The worst she can say is no."

I wasn't so sure about that. My mom could say quite a few things besides 'no' that would be worse. She could say that my father was a thief or a murderer. She could say he was a psychopath on death row. Or she could say that he had abused her, although I couldn't imagine Desiree taking abuse from anyone.

"All I knew for certain was that my mother, who sometimes told me way more than I wanted to know about the men she was dating, refused to say a word to me about the person who had contributed half of my DNA.

And yet, the deep concern Lucas expressed about Samuel's daughters growing up without a father had me wondering if now that I'm an adult, she might allow me to put that question to rest once and for all. It had been years since I'd broached the subject. I decided I would ask her one more time.

It's a little hard to know when to call my mom because I rarely know exactly where she is on the planet, and often the time zones between us are wildly separate.

After we got home, Lucas went straight to his *Daadi Haus* and before I could change my mind, I called her. This time I got lucky. She answered on the second ring. Plus, she was wide-awake and in a good mood.

"And where are you today, Mother?" I asked.

"I'm in Rome, Darling," she said. "Didn't I tell you?"

"No, you did not," I said. "Are you alone, by any chance?"

"Of course not." She spluttered out a laugh at the mere thought of being alone. "I'm with Phillipe, of course."

I knew Phillipe. He was the French hotelier to whom she had tried to talk me into selling Rick's home when I first inherited it. He'd had big plans for developing my property—which I rejected. Phillipe was a bit of a surprise, a dapper little man, the opposite of my mom's type. The men she favored tended to be tall and rugged looking. Since I couldn't imagine him as someone Desiree would make even a semi-permanent fixture in our lives, I hadn't given him much thought.

"How's the farm?" Desiree asked, her voice tight despite the casual question.

"Beautiful this time of year," I said. "The Amish have been so helpful."

There was that familiar pause—the same one that always followed any mention of the Amish.

"I don't know how you can stand to live there," she said.

"You mean because of the Amish? They're just people, Mom."

"They're not just people," she snapped, then caught herself. "I just meant—they're so different. It makes me nervous to be around them."

The conversation moved on, but her reaction lingered in my mind.

I decided I'd explore it later. Right now, I had other things on my mind.

"I need to talk with you about something important," I said. "I would prefer to do it when you're alone."

"Well, that sounds ominous," she said. "Are you all right?"

"I'm fine."

"Good. We're supposed to meet some friends in twenty minutes, and I've only managed to do one eye so far.

I knew what that meant. Desiree knew her way around a makeup kit. She was the queen of the smoky eye, but it took her a minimum of ten minutes to perfect one.

"This shouldn't take long." I drew a long breath as I gathered my courage. I could feel my pulse rate speed up and I felt a little dizzy trying to get the words out. "I want to know my father's name."

Silence.

"You won't shock me with anything you say. I don't care if my father is in a ward somewhere for the criminally insane. I just need to know."

Silence.

"It's time, Mother. It is not fair to keep this information from me."

I waited for an answer, but the phone went dead. When I tried to call back, my message went to voice mail, so I texted a message that would get my mother's attention.

"If you don't tell me who my father is, I'll find out, anyway. It might take me a day or a year, but if you force me to do that, I'll go straight to the tabloids when I find out. No, strike that. It would be better if I wrote a tell-all book. You know I can, and when I do, I promise the book won't be something your publicist can spin to make you look good."

Sometimes with my mom, you had to play hardball.

I tossed my phone on the kitchen table and stood at the kitchen window, watching the sun set over the fields. My heart was still racing over the fact I'd tried to confront my mother for the first time in years. My relationship with her had always been complicated. It was a mixture of love, exasperation, and a desperate, childish need for her approval that I'd never quite outgrown.

I'd spent years making excuses for her self-centeredness.

She's just focused on her career.

She had me so young.

That's just how artists are.

I'd constructed a narrative that painted her as flawed but well-intentioned.

But hanging up on me when I finally got up the courage to ask about my father again? That felt different. More deliberate. More hurtful.

I sighed. No matter how angry I felt, the pattern between us had always involved me ultimately forgiving her because, despite everything, she was the only family I had.

Until now, perhaps. It struck me that it wasn't my mother who had brought me soup when I was sick last month—it was Erma. It wasn't Desiree who kept the fire going in the fireplace, or who brought me fresh vegetables from the garden and stayed to chat—it was Lucas.

If I were in an accident, it wouldn't be my mother who came to the hospital, especially if she were on location somewhere for yet another movie. The most I could hope for would be if she remembered to have her assistant send me a fruit basket.

Some people were lucky enough to be born into loving, nurturing families. Others had to piece together "found families" from good friends and supportive neighbors.

Until moving to Sugarcreek, I'd never given such things much thought. As a child, I'd lived inside the books I read, put up with whatever living situation Mom chose for us, and eventually when I grew up, I'd lived inside the lives I wrote about.

The closest thing to an actual father I'd ever had was Rick Downey, Mom's third husband, the man who had left me this farm. For six years of my childhood, he'd been my rock, until Mom tired of him. Their divorce, which happened when I was twelve, had been devastating.

For the first time, I realized Rick hadn't just left me two hundred valuable acres, a farmhouse, and an antique store in the middle of Ohio. He had left me his own "found family" that he'd pieced together after the divorce. Knowing Desiree as well as he did, I had a feeling he must have known how much I would someday need it.

CHAPTER 10

Three days later, I was still pondering the mystery of Samuel's disappearance while I tried to feed the chickens. This was difficult to do without getting Zedekiah, the crazy mean rooster, riled up. Lucas sometimes offered to turn Zedekiah into chicken stew, but I kept saying no. As much as I disliked that rooster, he protected the flock from predators. I just wish he didn't consider me one of them.

We had heard nothing about Samuel, although Rachel checked in with us from time to time to see if we'd found out anything. With no license tags to run, no credit or debit cards to flag, and no cell phone to track, the police didn't have much of a trail to follow. We didn't even know what clothes Samuel was wearing, except it was something he hadn't left home with. I wondered how the police had ever tracked people down before cellphones and credit cards.

I had never thought about it before, but if an Amish man wanted to disappear, all he had to do was shave his beard, cut his hair, and put on *Englisch* clothes. If he did that, even his own children wouldn't recognize him. He could fade into the woodwork of society with no one giving him a second glance, especially if he were of the younger generation. I had noticed that it was mainly the older Amish people who still had that telltale Germanic lilt to their speech. The younger generations were losing it.

Lucas had been spending as much time with Gretchen and the children as possible. This was a sacrifice of time on his part that we could not afford because there was such an enormous amount of work to do on the farm in early spring.

Often, if I was working late, which I frequently did, I would see the light in his house glowing earlier and earlier as he tried to catch up on our farm chores so that he could help Gretchen with hers. She was still pregnant with her baby, and the pains were no longer bothering her, but we didn't know when they might start up again. She was trying to rest as much as possible.

I had started feeding and watering the chickens and collecting the eggs, because it was something I could do to help.

I was just finishing up when Lucas rode Midnight, his black stallion, back from Gretchen's house. My heart always felt lighter when Lucas came home. I thought about going to greet him so I could inquire about Gretchen, but he ignored me and took the horse straight to the barn.

He spent a long time there. I heard noises I had never heard coming from that barn before, so I brought my laptop out to the porch and pretended to work. That way, if he needed to talk, he could. If he didn't, he could pretend he didn't see me.

An hour later, he emerged from the barn and came striding through the yard, straight toward me. He looked like he'd been in a fight, but I knew that was impossible. There was no one in that barn for him to fight with except himself. The knuckles on both hands were skinned and bleeding from where he'd punched something. From the sounds I'd heard, I was guessing he'd taken out his frustration with Samuel by battering the barn wall.

He didn't sit on the top step of the porch as much as he sort of fell onto it. Every movement he made telegraphed disgust.

"He sent her a money order."

I didn't understand. "What?"

"Samuel sent Gretchen a money order for three hundred dollars."

"Today?"

"She received it in the mail while I was there."

I digested this unexpected news. "Where did the money come from?"

He shrugged. "Who knows?"

"Was there a note?" I prodded. "Some way for her to get in touch with him?"

"No. It was just the money order."

I closed my laptop. All pretense of working gone. "Do money orders say where they were sent from?"

"This one did," he said.

"And?"

"He bought it at a Walmart in Cleveland." He cradled his damaged right hand with his left one. "Cleveland is a big city."

"How did Gretchen react?"

"She's relieved that Samuel is alive. Confused and hurt by what he's done, but trying to act like everything is okay for the girls' sake. She's assured them their daett will be home soon."

"How can she say that when she doesn't know?"

"If he doesn't, I'll get his brothers to go with me, and we'll drag him back. We cannot allow him to abandon his family."

"How will you find him?"

He took his hat off, sat it on his knee, and ran his damaged hands through his hair with frustration. "I don't know."

"Did you tell the police?"

"I told Rachel. She was glad to know he's alive. A grown man who is sending money back home to his family is not something they are going to worry about. The police have taken him off the missing list."

I opened my laptop, typed in Cleveland, Ohio, and saw that it was a city of over three hundred thousand people. If Lucas went up there with nothing to go on but a money order from Walmart, he'd have his work cut out for him.

I wondered if Samuel knew the toll his actions were taking on others.

"If Samuel doesn't want to be found," I said, as gently as I could. "I don't think a few Amish men walking around the streets of Cleveland are going to find him. There's no guarantee he's even still there."

Lucas's shoulders slumped. "I know."

It was hard watching him feel so defeated. I wanted to help, but there wasn't much I could do.

"I'll go get some ice for those hands," I said. "It might help keep the swelling down."

His voice was flat. "*Danki.*"

CHAPTER 11

LUCAS

Lucas awoke to the sound of rain pattering on the roof. As a farmer, this made him happy. The young plants he had placed in the ground this past week could use a good drink. Then, as he lay in his bed, staring into the early dawn darkness, the rain drummed against the roof, intensifying until it became a roar.

This was decidedly not good. Not only could the tender plants be flattened by this sort of onslaught of water, but he now had another worry. The roof of Rick's old antique store in town was not in great shape. Lucas had planned on getting some friends together to help him replace it as soon as it looked like he might have a few days of dry weather.

If this rain didn't let up soon, he'd need to go check on things. There were too many valuable objects on that third floor to ignore the possibility of leaks.

A rare feeling of defeat hit him. It seemed like no matter how hard he worked; he kept falling farther behind. Having to shoulder Samuel's duties didn't help. He felt like an old horse that had been pulling a load too heavy for him for way too long.

He had been foolish to allow his frustrations to boil over yesterday

—to where he'd slammed his fists repeatedly against the barn walls! What had he been thinking? He flexed his hands, feeling the bandages Amy had placed on them tighten against the wounds he'd given himself.

Amy was shocked to see the intensity of his anger yesterday. He could see it in her eyes. He'd shocked himself, actually. He hadn't realized how frustrated and angry he'd become until he stopped pounding the wall and saw the results of what he'd done.

But it was not his way to stay in bed when there was work to do. He threw the covers off and stepped onto the polished wooden floor, making a mental list of what he needed to accomplish today.

He dressed while listening to the torrent of rain. It wasn't letting up. He'd better go check on the antique store. The roof was old. He feared for the possibility of leaks. He'd seen some discoloration on the ceiling the last time he'd been there. Rick had meant to hire a company to put a new roof on the place. Then Rick died, and it just hadn't gotten done. Going over there this morning to make certain the rain wasn't ruining everything on the third floor had become his priority of the day.

As Lucas unlocked the back door to the one-hundred-year-old antique store, he wondered what Amy would finally decide to do with it. The place was packed wall to wall with treasure and trash. The trick of running it as a viable business, though, was going to be discerning which was which. Rick had been an appraiser at Sotheby's, so there was definitely some treasure here. He also had an interesting sense of humor about his store and was not above hiding something like a baseball card worth a thousand dollars inside a cracked cookie jar worth maybe a dollar.

Lucas had seen customers unearth a first edition children's book worth a couple hundred dollars from an antique bureau drawer otherwise filled with mismatched bed sheets. Rare vintage clothing might be tossed into a trunk filled with children's stuffed animals.

He never knew if Rick made any real money from his store, but people loved coming to it, and Rick loved people, so it worked out.

For now, Amy was keeping it locked up—to everyone's disappointment. As a precaution, Lucas made it a habit to stop by once a week to check on things. Old roofs could leak, pipes could freeze, and small boys could throw stones through windows.

Rick kept used couches, comfy chairs and bookcases filled with old books on the main floor toward the front of the store. There was even a working fireplace he had kept blazing in cold weather. From the sidewalk, the place practically begged people to come in, sink down onto a couch, and lose themselves in a book or conversation.

This was not an accident. Rick had known exactly what he was doing. Tourists, grateful for a comfortable place to sit for a while and rest their aching feet, nearly always purchased something before they left.

He moved aside the closed curtains on the antique store's large display windows just enough to watch the rain pattering against the sidewalk. From a farmer's perspective, the timing of the rain couldn't be better. Spring planting was finished. His two Belgians were having a day off after all their hard work. He, however, didn't get days off very often.

He enjoyed being in the antique store, especially when it was closed. The couches, electric floor lamps, and overstuffed chairs in this store created such a different environment than what he was used to in his own spartan home. The idea of coming here, forgetting his responsibilities for a day, and quietly reading a book was a tempting one. There was even a working fireplace against one wall, in which he had logs and kindling stacked and ready. Because of the rain, there was a chill in the air. A wood fire would feel good and might dry things out a bit. All it would take was the touch of a match to create a nice, warm, blaze.

But he had more pressing things to do than keep a fire going. He grabbed the mop and mop bucket out of the small closet where Rick had kept housekeeping supplies. Then he started up the stairs, dreading what he might find up there.

The third floor wasn't as bad as he'd feared, but not as good as he'd hoped. The discoloration on the ceiling that he'd noticed last time he'd been here had definitely developed into a leak—steadily drip dripping onto the roll of ancient, scuffed, linoleum Rick had spread out on the floor several years earlier and then never moved it again. So far, the rainwater was contained on the linoleum—a giant puddle in the middle of the floor. He quickly mopped it up and then placed a mop bucket beneath to catch future leaks.

He examined the rest of the ceiling for other leaks and found none. He sat down in a caned rocking chair and watched the drips as he made plans With any luck, after the rain stopped, he should be able to do a quick patch job that would hold long enough for him to make arrangements to re-roof the whole building.

The rain continued to pour down, and the mop bucket continued to catch drips. As soon as it was nearly full, He found an old ceramic chamber pot, sat it beneath the leak, went to a window, and emptied the mop bucket out the window. Then he reset the larger bucket beneath the leak and moved the chamber pot until next time the mop bucket needed to be emptied.

It occurred to him that as long as it continued to rain; he was effectively imprisoned inside the store. He guessed he was going to have to take a day off after all. There were things he'd rather do than babysit a leak on a rainy day—but if this was the task the Lord had given him today, he guessed this was what he would do.

CHAPTER 12

I was surprised to see Lucas's horse and buggy tied at the shelter behind the antique store. He hadn't mentioned having plans to do any work there today, so I was a little surprised to see him there, but I was pleased. I had been intending to pick up a set of jade green salt and pepper shakers for the house I'd seen on the second floor of the antique store. I thought the vintage set would look pretty on my kitchen table.

However, I'd been putting off picking them up because I was reluctant to go into the store alone ever since discovering a stranger living there right before Christmas. If Lucas was already here, this was a good opportunity to go in without thinking someone was going to jump out at me.

I'd gotten a few much-needed groceries, but nothing that would spoil if I stopped in for a few minutes. I grabbed my umbrella and made a dash for the back door. It wasn't locked, but Lucas was nowhere to be found—at least not on the first floor.

"Hello?" I called. "Lucas?"

No answer.

I walked up the creaking wooden stairs, hoping he'd appear soon.

It was on the third floor I found him, sitting in a rocking chair, staring into space, looking about as morose as I'd ever seen him.

"What's going on?" I asked.

He startled. With all the noise the rain was making on the roof, he hadn't heard me call for him. It was probably just wishful thinking on my part, but he seemed to light up when he saw me.

"I'm making certain this bucket doesn't overflow." He stood and motioned for me to take his chair. I shook my head. There were plenty of places to sit. I grabbed one of those colorful metal chairs that I'd seen in old photos of Florida motels and dragged it over closer to him

We both sat for a while, silently, just watching the drip form on the ceiling, and then fall into the bucket with a small splash. It was oddly fascinating.

"You're a real fun date, Lucas Hershberger," I joked. "I don't know when I've had such a good time."

He nodded, as though he was taking my comment seriously. "When the rain stops, I'll put a tarp on the roof over that hole, and then we can go home and watch the grass grow."

I laughed, and he smiled at me. Although I would never admit it to anyone—watching the grass grow, or a leak drip into a bucket with Lucas Hershberger, beat the few dates I'd been on with other men, which wasn't saying a lot about my love life, but there you go.

"I think you're kinda stuck here," I said.

"I am." He lifted the bucket up and then slid the little white ceramic pot where it had been. "Why did you stop by?"

"There is a vintage salt and pepper set I wanted to take home with me." It sounded lame even to my own ears, so I confessed the actual truth. "I saw your horse and buggy and wanted to see if you were okay. You weren't in good shape last night."

"I know." He tossed the rainwater out the window, brought the bucket back, and started the process all over again. The bandages I'd put on his hands last night were gone, and I could see the damage he'd done. Some men would have taken that kind of frustration out on the nearest person—which, in this case, would have been me. Instead, Lucas had taken it out on an inanimate object, even though he'd hurt himself.

"Have you had lunch?" I asked.

"I didn't even have breakfast," he said. "I ran over here first thing, for fear there would be too much damage if I waited."

"I just got groceries. I have the fixings for ham and cheese sandwiches in the car. Want me to go bring it in?"

"Yes." He took a long look at the mop bucket. "I think that's empty enough that it will hold things for a while. Let's go downstairs."

My umbrella was still where I'd left it beside the door. Lucas opened it and held it over me while I rummaged around in the trunk of my car, getting our lunch. We brought it all in, and I sat things on a coffee table near the fireplace.

"You're cold." He rummaged around on the mantel until he found a box of kitchen matches. "I'll start a fire."

"That sounds good!"

Unfortunately, the box was empty.

"I'll go check Rick's office," he said.

CHAPTER 13

LUCAS

Lucas got the key from its hiding place beneath the counter and opened the door to Rick's private office. He rummaged through the desk, trying to find something with which to light the fire. It was a massive desk, extremely ornate with much expert hand carving. It had more pigeonholes than he'd ever seen and so many drawers that he marveled Rick had remembered where he put anything. Although a few people had asked to buy it, Rick let everyone know it wasn't for sale.

"Lunch is ready," Amy's voice interrupted his search.

Lucas swiveled around in Rick's chair. "Great."

Amy smiled, but she was hugging herself and shivering slightly. He'd noticed that she looked especially nice today. She wore a top he'd never seen before. It was a pale shade of yellow, modest enough but so thin and silky he figured she was regretting her choice of clothing on this chilly spring day.

Rick had always kept a wool cardigan sweater hanging from a hook behind the door. Lucas rose to get it for her. "You're cold," he said, and helped her into it.

"Thank you." Gratefully, she snuggled into the sweater, then she became distracted by Rick's desk.

"Well, hello there, old friend!" She stroked the top of the desk. "I remember this beauty well. I didn't know it was in here."

"This office is the only room in the store Rick kept locked. You and I were never here long enough to get the key and open it up."

"I have good memories about this desk," she said. "It was the one he used when he worked at Sothebys. Sometimes he took me to work with him, back when he was still married to my mom. He had a drawer he kept stocked with peppermint Life Savers."

She slid open a small drawer in the upper left corner of the desk as though she hoped there might still be a treat for her in the drawer, but it was empty.

"Rick's employers allowed you to visit him at work?" Lucas asked.

"I don't know if they formally allowed it, but he took me along with him sometimes anyway and I was happy to go. No one seemed to pay any attention. Sometimes I'd play beneath it. In fact, one day I found a hidden drawer under there. Rick hadn't known about it. It was a big day for me when I showed him."

"Was there anything in it?"

"There was! A silver dollar from 1861, a man's gold ring, and a stack of confederate money. Very exciting for a six-year-old."

She smiled at the memory, and Lucas saw a glimpse of the little girl she'd been when Rick took care of her.

"What happened to them?"

"Rick, let me keep all of it. He had bought the desk from a dealer in Alabama and said the desk had come from one of the plantations there. I got quite a history lesson that day."

"Do you want to check in that drawer?"

"Maybe another time." She glanced down at the dark opening beneath the massive desk. "It's probably empty, too."

Lucas spied a cigarette lighter beneath some papers and flicked it to see if it worked. It did.

He lit the fire and got it burning, then ran back up to the third floor to empty the bucket yet again. The rain was slacking off a bit. There would be enough time to enjoy Amy's lunch between throwing buckets of water out the window.

He had never considered himself a romantic. But he had to admit —there were a lot worse ways for a man to spend his time than having a makeshift picnic with a lovely woman, in front of a blazing fireplace, with rain pouring down outside.

This day that he had started with so much frustration and weariness of spirit had turned itself around remarkably. It was humbling.

"Thank you, Lord." His heart filled with gratitude as he went down to the second floor to grab the jade green salt and pepper set she'd mentioned. He'd noticed it, too, and she was right. It would look nice in her kitchen.

CHAPTER 14

The rain stopped while I was driving back to the farm. I had just gotten home and was feeding the chickens, when suddenly, with no warning, my globe-trotting mother chose to pay a visit.

It's hard to describe my mother's personality. I can't say that she's a pure narcissist, because she does do good things for people. But most of the time, she's spectacularly unaware of other people's needs and feelings. When they were going through their divorce, I overheard Rick tell Desiree she was "certifiably selfish." I love my mother, but I think Rick nailed it.

Desiree never calls to let me know when she's going to show up. It's a matter of pride for her. She prefers the freedom to come and go at will, and it's up to everyone else to deal with her sudden arrivals and departures. She blithely assumes she is welcome anywhere she goes—and because she's beautiful, rich, and can sometimes be a lot of fun, she usually is.

I've mentioned to her I'd really appreciate some warning before she comes for a visit, and it changes nothing. Unless she's in front of a camera, Mom is like a precocious two-year-old doing exactly as she pleases—while everyone stands around talking about how adorable she is.

Except for me. It isn't easy being raised by a toddler, no matter how adorable. I had to grow up fast.

Taxis don't exactly grow on trees out here in Amish country, but Desiree didn't seem the least bit concerned about making the taxi driver come all the way from the Cleveland Airport to my house. As she got out of the vehicle, I heard her instruct the driver to wait.

I tossed the last handful of chicken feed toward the flock. Since it had only just stopped raining, the chickens were looking damp and bedraggled. I suppose I did, too. Mom almost always caught me looking at my worst. It was almost uncanny. I'd stopped making excuses years ago.

"Hello mother." I brushed off my hands. "If I'd known you were coming, I'd have baked a cake."

She knew I was being sarcastic. Desiree does not eat cake or much of anything else with any caloric value.

"I need to talk to you." She was not smiling, and it was obvious she was not happy to see me.

"Am I in trouble, Mother?"

"Can we go on the porch?" she asked, already headed toward it.

"Of course." We walked to the house, where she took a seat on the porch swing.

"I'm parched," she said. "Do you have something to drink?"

"I have lemonade."

She looked hopeful. "Is it sugar free?"

"No."

"Oh." She sounded disappointed. "Ice water then?"

"I'll get it."

She drained the glass I brought her before she spoke again. "This water tastes funny. Is it from a well?"

"Yes."

"I hate well water."

80

"I'm fresh out of Evian right now, so we'll just have to struggle along."

She gave me a dirty look, then glanced around at my farm and sort of wrapped her arms around herself.

"This place gives me the heebie-jeebies," she said. "I really wish you would sell it."

"We've been through this before. I love it here. Why does it bother you so much?"

"How can you love living in a place where there are so many, I don't know, Amish people living around you?"

To my surprise, she shivered when she said the word "Amish."

"They've been good to me."

"I think they're creepy."

"Mom!" I wasn't sure what was wrong with her, but she was definitely in a mood. "You shouldn't say things like that! You didn't think Lucas was creepy when you met him. You tried to flirt with him."

"Lucas is a hunk," she said. "He doesn't count. The younger men aren't so bad, but the older ones with their scraggly beards and weird haircuts..."

I couldn't believe what I was hearing. Desiree had friends who would make the everyday Amish person look like the soul of normality. Her visceral-like prejudice against my neighbors was strange.

"Except for Lucas, when have you ever even been around any Amish? To my knowledge, the Amish don't spend a lot of time in L.A."

"You don't know what I've been around." She gave me a dark look. "You've always had it so easy."

I gasped at that statement. It was incredibly unfair. I'd spent much of my childhood sitting in various bars, waiting for Desiree to finish singing, or later in some movie set trailer, wishing we could go home —but not entirely sure where home was. Maybe that's why this place meant so much to me. It had practically shouted "home" from the moment I'd seen it.

"That's not fair, Mom." I said. "Have you been drinking?"

"No," she said. "I've been too busy trying to track down that man you're so desperate to meet."

"And?" My heart was pounding so hard I could hear it.

"I found him."

"He's alive?"

She didn't answer at first. Instead, she rattled the ice cubes in her glass and sipped a couple more drops from the melting ice. I could tell she was nervous, a rare emotion for her. Desiree was nothing if not self-assured.

"He is most definitely alive."

I felt dizzy. A lifetime of wondering and hoping, and finally I was on the verge of knowing who my father was. At least that's what I hoped would happen. Desiree could turn on an emotional dime. It made her a superb actress, but a worrisome mother.

"So, you're finally ready to tell me," I said.

"No," she said, irritably. "I'm not at all ready. But I'm sick of you nagging me about it. Honestly! I don't understand why you can't just let it go. My marriage to him was a mistake. I put it behind me a long time ago.

"Does that also make me a mistake?" I waited. It would not be unlike her to admit it. Desiree could lie with ease, but sometimes she could also be chillingly honest.

"No." Her voice softened. "I've never regretted having you."

It felt good to hear her say that. Then her voice turned bitter, and she ruined it.

"… until you called and threatened to go public with my private life!"

"You always said there was no such thing as bad publicity."

"Not always. It depends. You know how much I value my privacy."

I stared at her in amazement. She was lying. Whether to me or to herself, it didn't matter.

"No, you don't," I said. "You always said privacy is overrated."

"That's usually true," she said. "But I've tried to keep my relationship with your father out of the public eye."

"Why?"

"It's a long story," she said, looking older than I'd ever seen her. This thing about my father had really taken a toll, and I couldn't imagine why. She had dated and married so many men. What made him any different?

It was an especially warm day for spring now that the rain had stopped. I would have felt sorry for the taxi driver sitting in the car, except I could hear the motor running, and knew both the meter and air conditioner were probably going full-tilt.

Needing a moment to collect myself, I took my mother's glass of melting ice cubes and went inside to refill it. When I returned, she had changed her mind about the swing. Now, she was curled up in my favorite wicker chair and was wrapped in a blanket I kept there.

The blanket was a deep blue and made of soft wool. That she was cuddled inside of it, despite the warm weather, was an interesting sign. When she was feeling vulnerable, she always covered herself with some kind of blanket, despite the temperature. This situation had obviously shaken her. Sometimes silence was the best policy with my mother, so I sat on the swing and waited.

Like most kids who don't know their father, I had made up stories about him in my mind. As an adult, I still did. Was he a CIA agent? Married politician? Russian spy?

She picked a piece of lint off the blanket, avoiding looking at me. "So, after your phone call, I flew home to New York."

"That was quick."

"Phillippe owns a private jet," she said.

"Of course he does."

Desiree glanced at me, then back down at her hands, which continued to pick at the blanket. "After you called, Phillipe convinced me that now that you're an adult, you do have the right to know who your father is."

"Good for him." I made a note to thank Phillipe. There was more to him than I'd thought.

"When I got back to New York City, I hired a woman who specializes in tracing people. She is quite expensive, by the way."

"Let me guess," I said. "After you gave her the information, she found him in about fifteen minutes on her computer."

"Actually, it took thirty." My mother sounded irritated. "She always charges me way too much for no more time than she spends."

"You've used her before?"

"You don't think I would waste my time dating a man without doing a complete background check first, do you?"

"Of course not." I didn't allow myself to be distracted. "So, she found him?"

"She did."

"And?"

"His name is Brady."

Brady. I tilted my head backward and stared at the porch ceiling. Tears pooled in my eyes as I savored it. My father had a first name, and I liked it.

"When did you take the tree swing down?" Mom pointed at a gigantic oak in my front yard.

"What swing?" I asked. "I never had a tree swing."

"My mistake," Mom said. "I thought I'd seen one there."

Her attempt to distract me was irritating, and it would not work.

"Why have you kept my father a secret from me all these years?"

"I'm telling you about him now, aren't I?"

I sighed. "Do you suppose you could tell me his last name as well?"

"Maddox. His name is Brady Maddox."

I liked his last name as well. I was a Maddox. So far, so good.

"Where does he live?"

"Oh, all over the place, I suppose," Desiree said.

Images of a CIA agent father came to mind.

"And what does he do that takes him all over the place?" There was a shiver of excitement in my voice. I couldn't wait to hear more.

"You are going to be so disappointed," Desiree said. "I don't know what you've been imagining, but your father is nothing special."

"I don't care what he is," I said. "I just want to know him."

"It's good that you don't care what he is." Mom turned her head, but her eyes slanted up at me, like they do when she's holding a secret that she knows I won't want to hear. "He's a clown"

The word "clown" was one of the many dismissive words Mom used when she was referring to a man she didn't like.

"I don't care what you think of him, Mom. What does my father do?"

"That's his job, dear." Desiree gave me an amused look. "He works as a clown."

CHAPTER 15

"You're joking," I said.

"I am not," Desiree said.

The image of my father as a CIA agent evaporated.

I try not to be judgmental, but I have to admit that the news of his choice of employment was a bit of a letdown.

"What kind of clown?"

"Does it matter?" Desiree said. "I suppose he's the kind that wears a funny hat and a red nose and makes people laugh. I didn't ask for details."

I stewed over this for a moment. "So, you are saying that Desiree Stanton's first husband was a clown? That doesn't sound like your style at all."

"Actually, I was a little surprised to find this out myself," she confessed.

I gathered up my nerve to ask the question that had burned within me most of my life. "Why hasn't my father ever tried to contact me?"

"Oh, that." Mom paused. "He has no idea you ever existed."

Somehow, I'd always envisioned a scene where he walked out on us, or mom walked out on him with me in her arms. "Why?"

"I left him before I even knew I was pregnant with you. It turned out to be for the best. Everything was simpler that way. No fighting over custody. No awkward visitation issues. You belonged entirely to me."

I knew Desiree could be self-centered, but she still had the ability to shock me. Had it never occurred to her how her decision might affect me? Did she even care?

"It's water under the bridge, darling." She flitted her fingers in the air like she was shooing away unwanted memories. "Your father and I were over a long time ago."

"So, do I have grandparents on his side who are still living? Other siblings?" I could hardly wrap my mind around the possibility. It had just been me and Mom for so long. She'd always told me we didn't have any living relatives.

"How should I know?" she said. "Once I got away from him, I never looked back."

"Why did you leave him? Was he mean to you?"

"Never," Desiree said. "He had… other problems."

"Like wanting to become a clown?"

"Well, no. I think he must have become a clown after he got out of prison."

I felt my heart thud. "Prison? Wait. What?"

"Miss Stanton?" The taxi driver interrupted us, looking worried. "My daughter has a piano recital tonight. If we leave right now, I might make it."

My mother was seldom accommodating, but this time, she jumped at the chance. It was unsettling. I needed more information, but Desiree was done. The little daughter's piano recital was as good an excuse as any.

"I want to meet my father," I said.

Desiree typed something into her cell phone. My phone dinged, I looked, and there was an address.

"Brady does gigs all over the U.S., but it looks like he spends a good bit of his time right here in Ohio. In fact, he's working at a place up near the Akron/Cleveland area this evening. If you are absolutely determined to see him, tonight is as good a time as any."

My father was in Ohio!

"Please, Mom," I pleaded. "Will you stay and go with me?"

"Oh, sweetie." She smiled and patted my cheek. "Of course not."

"But how will I know him? Do you have a picture?"

She busied herself by folding the blanket. "I guess you could just keep an eye out for a clown who answers to the name of Brady."

"Okay. I guess." I felt a little shaken at the thought of going to see him with so little time to prepare. What if he didn't like me? What if I didn't like him? What if he closed the door in my face—assuming he had a door to close? I did not know what sort of living arrangements clowns had.

"Now, promise me you won't go public about this," Mom said. For a moment, she looked a little scared. "I've got to be especially careful about my reputation right now. I've been asked to audition for a good part in a Ron Howard movie. If any of this comes out, it might blow my chances."

"If any of what comes out?" I asked. "Are you ashamed of my father?"

"There's nothing wrong with Brady Maddox." She finished folding the blanket and handed it to me. "There never was."

"Then what are you afraid of?"

"There are things from my past that will be judged and discussed by people who can't possibly understand... including Phillipe."

"You really care about him that much?"

"He makes me feel safe."

I couldn't argue with that. Feeling safe was no small thing. "I won't say anything."

"Promise?"

"I promise," I said. "Thanks for the information, Mom."

"One more thing. Phillipe is still interested in this property. Are you sure you don't want to sell it? If you sold it and moved back to New York City, you could live a glamorous life in a much better apartment."

I wondered what my mother had against this property, anyway. She'd been trying to talk me into selling it since the moment she saw it. There was nothing wrong with this place. Nothing! Except that it was... home. To me.

"I like it here, Mom. I'm not selling," I said. "And I seriously need for you to quit trying to make me."

"I need to go." My mother took a deep breath, and then right before my eyes, she stopped being "mom" and turned into Desiree Stanton. All whirling scarves, gold jewelry, colorful skirt, heart-stopping smile, and that perfect mane of blonde hair. A beautiful dynamo, as usual. It was obvious that having deposited news she didn't want to give me, she couldn't wait to leave.

I didn't stop her. In fact, I said nothing except goodbye. I love my mother. I do. But sometimes dealing with her for any length of time is exhausting.

I looked up at the address she had given me. It was in Burbank, Ohio. Less than two hours away. The name of the place was unfamiliar to me, but I decided twenty-eight years was long enough to wait. I'd see if Lucas would go with me for moral support, but even if he didn't, nothing was going to keep me from trying to meet my father. Who knew? Maybe he was really a great clown.

CHAPTER 16

LUCAS

Lucas read a tattered Zane Grey western while he monitored the mop bucket. Then the rain stopped, the sun came out, and he fidgeted. Not only did he need to get a tarp fastened over the hole in the roof, but Gretchen and Samuel had twenty head of Angus cattle on their property this year, and he'd noticed one place where the fencing needed mending. If he didn't take care of it, before long the steers would get out, and have to be rounded up. People didn't appreciate having their neighbor's cattle stampeding through their yards and gardens.

He didn't mind mending fences, and he didn't mind helping his pregnant sister. What he did mind was the fact that Samuel should be here to take care of his own chores! But that was becoming old news.

If a job needed doing, Lucas was hard-wired to go do it. That was his way. He seldom put off anything until tomorrow if there was still daylight enough to do it today. While he waited for the roof to dry enough to be less dangerous to walk on, he'd drop by Gretchen's to check on her and the girls and tighten up that drooping fence corner while he was there.

He needed to lock Rick's office before he left, but then he remembered what Amy had said about a hidden drawer beneath the desk and grew curious. He wondered where a master furniture maker might have hidden such a drawer. He wanted to investigate before he locked up.

Pulling the desk chair away from the desk, he crawled beneath and looked. He found no sign of a hidden drawer. He crawled back out, grabbed a flashlight from a nearby shelf, and wedged himself back under. There, hidden close to the bottom of the right side, was the hint of a rectangular cut. He could see no knob to pull, so he pushed and felt it give just enough to pop back out as though spring loaded.

He glimpsed something inside and pulled it the rest of the way out. Reaching in, he grasped three sheets of handwritten paper and saw that he'd discovered a letter from Rick to Amy.

Then he noticed the date written at the top was fairly recent, only a few months before Rick had died. It was three carefully handwritten pages. He quickly scanned the first page.

Dear Amy,

I found out today that I have a heart condition. The doc says I need to be careful. What that tells me is that I'd better be getting my affairs in order. If you are reading this, you will have already inherited my estate.

I suppose you might simply sell it all and never read this letter. But I think you'll see this old desk and remember having played beneath it, and you'll remember this drawer and the fun you had discovering it and its secret stash. I'm betting on you wanting to see it again, maybe even hoping I might have left something in it for you to find.

(By the way, those coins, confederate money and ring were all deposited by me—hoping you'd find the secret drawer and that the discovery would become a lovely memory for you. Crafty way to get you interested in history, wasn't it?)

I don't know what kind of impact this letter will have on you, but you are a grown woman now, and it is necessary to write this all down if I am to have any peace.

Lucas stopped reading. This letter was incredibly private, and he had no right to read it. In fact, he was embarrassed that he'd read this much. He debated taking the letter to her, but left it where Rick had hidden it. He'd tell her about it later.

He locked Rick's office door, made certain the fire in the fireplace was out, and left, mentally making a list of supplies he'd need in order to mend that fence of Samuel and Gretchen's.

CHAPTER 17

L ucas came home just as Mom was leaving. She blew a kiss at
him from the taxi window, which made him look uncomfortable. That summed up my mother and Lucas's relationship. She
flirted. He looked miserable. This would be funny if I wasn't worried
he would hold her actions against me.

"How is the store?" I asked as he approached.

"I got the roof fixed—at least temporarily. And I checked on
Gretchen and the girls."

"How are they?"

"The girls are fine. Gretchen is confused and hurt, but those early
labor pains have stopped, so the baby is okay for now. I got a weak
place in the fence mended."

I could tell Lucas was in a good mood, and I was glad because I had
a big favor to ask.

"Would you mind going with me to something tonight, Lucas?"

"What is it?"

I glanced down at the address my mother had texted me. "I'm not
exactly sure, but it's in Burbank, Ohio."

He gave me a quizzical look. "What is in Burbank?"

"According to my mother—my father."

He looked startled. "I thought you didn't know your father's name."

"I didn't. Now I do."

"Is this why she was here?" He glanced in the direction where the taxi had driven off.

"Yes," I said. "A surprise visit. So, can you go with me to meet him? I could really use a friend tonight."

"I suppose." He looked wistfully at the barn, as though longing to be there. "You should not have to face this alone."

I would have preferred a little more enthusiasm about spending time with me, but Lucas is honest to a fault. He didn't want to go do this, but he would.

Still, it was all I could do not to hug him; I was so grateful he'd agreed to go. Of course, had I hugged him, he would probably have run away. It might even have been the end of our friendship.

CHAPTER 18

I spent the next two hours getting ready to meet my father. While I showered and chose my clothes, I kept wondering what he would think of me and what I would think of him.

It wasn't easy choosing an outfit to meet a father who didn't know I existed. After I'd discarded about half a dozen outfits, I settled on a simple yellow sundress sprigged with tiny white daisies and a light denim jacket. I curled my hair, which was something I only saved for special occasions, and completed the look with simple pearl earrings.

By the time I finished, I'd worked myself up into a fine state of nerves.

I wondered if Lucas was ready yet. He had so much on his mind about his missing brother-in-law. I was afraid he might have forgotten what we were doing tonight. I went outside and sure enough; he was kneeling in the dirt, plastic ice cream bucket beside him, planting irises.

"We need to leave in a half hour," I said.

I watched the thought process on his face as he tried to remember why we needed to leave. "Oh. Your father. Right. I will be ready."

"Do I look okay, Lucas? I'm really nervous about this meeting."

Instead of answering, he planted the last bulb, took the garden hose, and gently watered the earth over them.

Then he turned the hose off, took a deep breath, and said, "I believe your father will see that you have taken much care with your appearance."

Huh?

I stared at him. "I curl my hair, apply makeup, wear my cutest dress, and that's the best you can do?"

He smiled apologetically. "You look nice, Amy. But complimenting one another's' physical appearance is something my people avoid. We dress plainly on purpose to avoid prideful thoughts."

"Oh."

A little embarrassed, I went back to the house to wait.

Less than thirty minutes later, he walked out of the *Daadi Haus*. He was showered and freshly clothed in a dark blue shirt, black pants, and black suspenders. His sleeves were neatly folded back to his elbows. He carried his black hat in one hand. His wet hair was combed straight back. I might have been mistaken, but it looked to me like he had even trimmed his beard a little.

He was tall, good-looking, and well-built. His blue eyes were intelligent and kind. He was one of the most capable men I had ever known. I couldn't help but wonder how long before some Amish woman would catch his eye. Erma told me it had been three years since his wife died. It was a wonder someone hadn't snatched him up already.

"You smell like sandalwood," I said, surprised, after we got into the car.

"A Christmas present. Soap from my youngest sister, Ellen." He sounded slightly embarrassed. "She drew my name and told everyone I would now have no excuse to smell of horse manure."

"It's nice."

"I will tell my sister thank you."

I started the car. We put our seat belts on. I think we both felt a little self-conscious. It was the first time we'd gone somewhere together dressed up.

"Does your father know you are coming to see him?" he asked.

"No," I said. "Mom says he doesn't know I exist."

Lucas pondered this. "It will not be easy for either of you."

"You think?" It sounded more sarcastic than I intended. I nervously chewed my thumbnail for a moment, tasted the sting of freshly applied fingernail polish, and resolutely gripped the steering wheel with both hands. Biting my nails was something I'd put behind me years ago—usually.

"You only bite your nails when you are worried," Lucas said. "Are you okay?"

"I'm afraid he won't like me."

When Lucas heard this, he turned in his seat and studied me. It made me nervous. I thought he might be ready to criticize my sundress, which was shorter than the Amish women wore. Instead, he said something that took my breath away.

"I think it would be very difficult for any man not to like you."

Seriously? Sometimes—rarely, but sometimes—Lucas uses the right words at the right time.

I blinked away tears as I backed out of the driveway.

"What is this place we are going to?" Lucas asked.

"It's named Buckin' Ohio," I said. "I checked them out online while I was getting ready. The website says they put on a lot of different events throughout the year. Tonight looks like some sort of rodeo."

"I will enjoy seeing that," Lucas said as he relaxed into his seat.

For the rest of the drive, we discussed the situation with his sister and her children, even though there wasn't really anything new to discuss.

When we arrived at Buckin' Ohio, an hour and a half later, Lucas insisted on paying for the tickets. He seemed to think it was a man's job to pay. He's old-fashioned that way. Of course, he's old-fashioned in pretty much every way, so it shouldn't come as a surprise.

We climbed into the stands and Lucas carefully seated himself a full foot away from me. There was a surprising number of Amish people in the crowd, so I suppose he didn't want to risk someone who knew him thinking he was there with an *Englisch* woman.

I could have really used a little hand holding, or even a reassuring arm around my shoulders, but that wasn't going to happen, and I didn't expect it to. It was enough that he had agreed to come with me. The crowd was loud and rowdy, but good-natured. Lots of children were there with their parents. All sorts of roping and riding went on. They even had a cute race for children involving stick horses. It would have been quite enjoyable had I not been nervously looking for a glimpse of my father.

Then the announcer said they would start the bull riding. At that moment, four clowns came prancing out, and the people cheered. I assumed one of them was my father, but how could I know which one?

"I've been to rodeos before, but I never cared for this part," Lucas said, leaning toward me. "I feel sorry for the rider and the bull."

I watched the young, whip-thin rider climb into the tight chute, then gingerly slide onto the bull. The four brightly dressed clowns stopped trying to amuse the crowd, took positions a few yards from the chute, and became deadly serious as they waited.

The audience grew quiet and tense. The announcer introduced the rider and the bull by name, and then the chute door opened, and a whirling dervish of a bull burst out with what looked like a life-sized rag doll on its back, except the doll was a man being slung this way and that while clinging to the rope wrapped around the bull's body. He held on while the crowd roared encouragement, and then the bull whipped around in the opposite direction and threw the young man off balance.

I could tell he was in trouble, and he knew it, too. The bull flung him off, then turned on him with hooves and horns, while the rider curled up into a fetal position, making himself as small a target as possible. The clowns threw themselves in front of the bull, distracting him, pulling his attention away from the rider lying on the ground.

The bull lowered his head and charged one of them, who ran for the fence and clambered on top of it for barely a split second before the bull slammed its massive head into it. The impact was so hard; it sounded like thunder.

The clown sitting on top of the fence comically fanned himself with his hat and wiped imaginary sweat off his forehead. Then, when the bull moved a few yards away, the clown jumped down into harm's way again and wiggled his bottom at the bull. Apparently, this was a signature move for him, because he'd painted a big red bull's-eye on the seat of his pants.

The bull pawed the ground, then lowered its head and came after him again. Once again, it hit the fence just as the clown vaulted over it.

By that time, the other clowns had successfully gotten the rider to safety, and other workers led the bull out of the arena. At that point, the rodeo workers readied themselves for the next rider.

Four more cowboys rode four different bulls as the animals tried different violent twists and turns to throw them off. Every muscle in my body knotted up, watching. This was a different world to me, and a dangerous one. If any of those clowns turned out to be my father, I worried he would be trampled to death before I ever got to meet him.

All the rides were worrisome, but the fifth one was the worst. The rider got bucked off, and his hand got caught in the rope he'd been holding. The bull turned into a tornado, whirling around and around with the rider's body swinging nearly parallel to the ground, unable to detach himself.

It was an impossible situation. The rider was entirely at the bull's mercy, and based on the wild eyes of that bull, there wasn't a drop of mercy in it. I was terrified that the rider was going to die. I couldn't imagine what could be done to stop this terrible thing.

Then I saw one clown streak toward the furious bull and the incapacitated rider. He leaped onto the animal and somehow clung to the bull's back while he sawed through the rope with a knife. This freed the rider, who fell unconscious to the ground. The beast reared up and began to pummel the unconscious rider with its hooves.

The clown who had cut through the rope dropped to the ground and, in one heart-stopping moment, threw his own body over the unmoving rider—protecting him from further damage by absorbing the blows from those vicious hooves. It was the bravest thing I'd ever seen.

This brought the crowd to its feet in one horrified gasp. I waited, nearly hyperventilating, until the other clowns could draw the bull's attention away, and men with ropes, on horseback, maneuvered it out of the ring.

Then I saw the clown who had been protecting the unconscious rider kneeling beside him, cradling him in his arms while he waited for the on-location emergency medical technicians to rush into the arena. It wasn't until the EMTs took over that the clown got to his feet.

The crowd, still standing, began chanting, "Brady! Brady! Brady!" as he limped toward the exit. Apparently, people who followed the rodeo circuit knew him by name.

I thought my heart would burst with pride. I had just witnessed the most heroic and self-sacrificing action in my life, and it was by my father!

"Is that him?" Lucas asked.

I nodded as my eyes filled and then overflowed with tears. Who needed a make-believe dad who was a CIA agent when my real flesh-and-blood father was capable of that?

CHAPTER 19

The rodeo was over after one more bull ride and people began melting away.

"Are you okay?" Lucas asked.

"I need to go see him," I said. "I'm not sure how to go about finding him, but now is the time to try."

"Then we should go." Lucas turned to lead the way, with me following.

There was none of that gentlemanly hand-at-the-small-of-my-back, like some other men do. The last thing Lucas wanted was to give anybody the impression that he and I were together. I wasn't sure what the ramifications would be for him within his church, but I didn't want to find out. I was afraid they might make him get a different job, so he wouldn't have to be around me so much.

He kept silent as we made our way toward the building where we saw cowboys and other rodeo people coming out. They seemed to be heading toward a cluster of RVs parked close together. Soon, I caught sight of the man I thought might be my dad. As a clown, he had worn grease makeup, and I hadn't been able to see his features, but he was the only one limping.

Cleaned up, this man was nice-looking. He was taller in person than he'd seemed earlier when he was running around the arena in floppy clown's clothes. Now, he wore a denim shirt, jeans, cowboy boots, and a large, silver and turquoise belt buckle. He had a rugged appearance that I liked.

"Excuse me," I said, walking up to him. "Are you Brady Maddox?"

"I was the last time I looked in the mirror." He grinned, all cowboy charm. "How can I help you, miss?"

I hesitated. Now that I was face to face with him, I wasn't entirely sure what words to use to tell him I thought he might be my father.

"That was a brave thing you did today," I said.

"Just part of the job." He shrugged and lost interest. Apparently, he was used to fans gushing over him.

"Did you ever know a Desiree Stanton?" I asked.

He focused and thought for a moment. "Can't say that I ever did. Name does sound kinda familiar, though."

"She's a movie star. She's been in a lot of films."

"I'm not much of a movie-goer." He began to sidle around me. "Now, if you'll excuse me."

"She says she was your wife."

"I've only been married once," he chuckled. "Pretty sure I'd remember if I'd been married to a movie star."

He started to move on but stopped.

"Who are you?" Suspicion flattened his voice. The good-old-boy persona disappeared.

"My mom says I'm your daughter."

It seemed to stagger him for an instant. He kind of reeled back, then he pulled himself together and his voice roughened. "If you're after money, miss, you're barking up the wrong tree. I'm not rich and I don't have a daughter."

"I'm not after money…" I could feel him edging away from me again.

"Excuse me," Lucas interrupted the conversation. "What was your wife's name?"

"She was Darla Sanders before we got married, but I haven't seen her since she walked out on me."

"How long ago was that?" I asked.

"Gosh, twenty-eight, maybe twenty-nine years ago." Brady looked closer at me, his eyes squinting against the setting sun. "How old are you?"

"I'm twenty-eight, sir," I said. "And there's a chance my mother changed her name after you two broke up. I never could find out the name of her first husband, and research is something I do for a living."

He seemed unsure about what to do. I held my breath, hoping he wouldn't walk away.

"Follow me," he said. "We'll talk in my RV."

CHAPTER 20

O nce we got inside his RV, I felt Brady's eyes studying me. "You do look a bit like my baby sister."

"I have an aunt?" I tried to keep the eagerness out of my voice.

"I didn't say Betty was your aunt," he said. "I just said you look like her. Most people look like other people."

"Okay," I said.

I silently vowed not to get too excited about this man, who was still trying to wrap his mind around the idea that I might be his daughter. We were seated in the living room area of his RV. To his credit, it was immaculate. To me, it looked like it was being kept by a man who had learned to live in close quarters, like on a ship... or in prison.

I sat on a small couch, Brady sat across from me, and Lucas had chosen to sit at the kitchen table, a few feet removed from us. I guess it was his way of trying to give us privacy.

Brady glanced at Lucas. "I'm sorry, but who are you again?"

"This is Lucas Hershberger," I said. "My business partner. He manages the farm I own in Sugarcreek. I didn't want to come alone."

Brady couldn't seem to sit still. He stood up to pace, which was a bit of a feat for a tall man in an RV. I noticed he was still favoring his left leg, and I knew it must hurt him. I tucked my legs beneath me to keep my feet out of his way. Those cowboy boots of his could do some damage if he stepped on my toes. He stopped pacing. "Do you have any pictures?"

"Of my mother? Of course."

I had dozens. Desiree was nothing if not photogenic. I dug into my purse and came out with my cell phone.

"Here." I showed him the most recent photo of her. She was standing on the deck of a yacht in a yellow bikini, wearing a gossamer-like white cover up blown back by an ocean breeze. She looked happy, gorgeous, and at least ten years younger than her actual age.

Brady took the phone, looked at the photo, and let out a low, nearly silent whistle.

He handed it back. "That can't be her. Darla was a brunette."

"Desiree is a brunette," I said. "She prefers being a blonde, though."

He took another long look. "That woman does resemble the woman I knew as Darla Sanders a little."

"Does your mother have a tattoo?" he asked.

"She has one."

"Where?"

"High on the front top of her right thigh, but small."

He pulled a piece of paper and a pencil out of a drawer and handed it to me. "Draw it."

I hadn't thought about the tattoo as any sort of proof. It had been such a long time since I'd seen it. In fact, she'd looked into having it removed, but as far as I knew, she had never done it.

Trying hard to remember details, I made a rough drawing of it and handed it to him.

Brady took it, looked at it, sank down onto the little couch across from me, threw his head back, and covered his eyes with one of his hands. I glanced at Lucas. He silently shook his head at me, as though warning me to keep quiet and let Brady work through whatever he had to work through.

So, I waited. It seemed to take forever, but Brady finally took his hand away and looked at me. His eyes were red rimmed and wet.

"That's Darla's tattoo. I've never seen one like it."

"I'm sorry," I said. "I didn't mean to bring back painful memories."

"Shoot. You didn't bring back painful memories, sweetheart," Brady said. "I always wanted a child, but it never worked out for me. Now that I'm a broken-up old man, here you are, sweet as sugar, trying to claim me as your daddy. Yeah, I'll take that deal. You look too much like the Maddox family to argue with it."

And with that, my father stood and wrapped me up in a hug so tight he nearly cracked my ribs. It takes a powerful man to fight bulls.

I could see Lucas's face over my dad's shoulder. He was watching with such a depth of compassion that it almost knocked the last bit of breath out of me.

When my father finally let go, it was like he wanted to do everything at once.

"We need to celebrate!" he said. "I'd take you two out for dinner if there was a good steakhouse around here still open."

"I'm fine, Brady." The sweet taste of the word "Dad" was on the tip of my tongue, but it was way too soon.

"Then something to drink! Are you thirsty? I got plenty of sodas. I'd offer something stronger, but I used to have a drinking problem and I don't want to fall off the wagon again. Last time I had alcohol, it started me on a bender that landed me in jail. Haven't had a drink since."

"What did you do that was bad enough to be sent to prison?" I asked, as he went to the fridge, popped the tabs on three cans of Cokes and handed them around.

"I did some stupid stuff. We can talk about all that later." He held the can in the air. "To having a daughter!" Then he hesitated. "What did you say your name is again?"

109

"Amy."

"To my daughter, Amy!" He tilted his head back and drained the can.

"Rodeo jobs are thirsty work," he said, wiping his mouth. "I always have to hydrate for a while afterward."

He grabbed another can from the refrigerator, sat down across from me again, and crossed his long legs. "So, where do we start?"

"I have no idea," I said. "I didn't even know your name until today."

"How's your mother?"

"You saw her picture," I said. "That was taken two weeks ago. She's fine."

"Married?"

"Not at the moment, but so far she's been married five times, counting you."

"None of them were legal, then," he said. "Except ours."

"What do you mean?"

"I mean, Darla just took off when she left me. She never got back in touch about a divorce. There were no papers to sign. Legally, I suppose we're still married."

"You can't be serious."

"I'm as serious as a funeral procession."

I glanced at Lucas again, who simply raised his eyebrows as though he wasn't sure what to think about it, either. This sort of scenario was definitely not part of his culture. He still sat at the kitchen table, watching our little tableau with interest.

"What happened?" I asked. "Why did Mom leave you?"

"She didn't tell you?"

"She did not."

"Are you sure you want to know?"

"I do."

"It won't make your mom look too good. I've never had a daughter before, so I'm not sure how much to tell you. I can make up a fairytale if you need me to."

"I don't need fairytales," I said. "What I need is the truth."

"Then where do you want me to start?" he said.

"Why did the two of you split up?"

"Why do you think?" he said.

I didn't want to make him mad, but I wasn't sure when I would get another chance to ask the questions I'd had for years. Now was my chance.

"I'm sorry to say this, and Mom never told me the reason she left, but the fact that she refused to talk about you gave me the impression that she had needed to run away from you to protect us."

Instead of defending himself, he started laughing.

"Why is that funny?" I said. "I don't understand."

"I loved Darla, and I treated her well. My whole family did. The reason I'm laughing is that you thought she ran away because she was in danger. The day she left, I couldn't even feed myself, let alone lift a hand to her."

CHAPTER 21

LUCAS

Nothing in Lucas's life could have prepared him for this moment. When he was a child, he had his father, two grandfathers, and a great-grandfather on his mother's side. He knew exactly who he was and who he came from. He'd taken having family in his life for granted—like the air that he breathed.

Now, seeing the raw hunger on Amy's face as she dealt with the immensity of meeting her father, he was ashamed he'd never realized that when it came to family, he was a rich man.

As Amy and her father talked, Lucas mentally totaled up his close relatives still living. Counting his sisters, brothers-in-law, aunts, uncles, nieces, and nephews, there were sixty-three. If he added first cousins, the number would be well over a hundred. He knew them all by name and liked most of them. They created a sort of safety net that he rarely thought about until he or they needed help.

Amy only had her mother.

He watched her, sitting there in her cute dress and denim jacket. Her eyes were alive with excitement over meeting her father. He'd seen those same eyes cloud over with anger when she had been approached about selling her land, and he'd watched them as she'd laughed at something funny Erma said or seen them alight with intel-ligence as she researched the books she wrote.

There was a steadiness to Amy that reminded him of good farm-land—rich with possibility, responsive to careful tending. But the most profound moment he'd ever experienced with her was today, when she began crying with relief over discovering that the coura-geous rodeo clown was her father.

Fortunately, he didn't recognize any of the Amish people who had attended the rodeo. The ribbons on the hats of the men were a little wider, and the women's dresses a little darker and longer, which showed that they were from a different sect than his. There was a good chance no one would recognize and report him to his bishop, but the Amish grapevine was a powerful force.

His people, unfortunately, probably had more reason to worry about his relationship with Amy than any of them realized. She had looked so sweet and vulnerable when she'd asked him if she looked okay, that he hadn't known what to say. His heart was too full of conflicting emotions, and so he'd said nothing.

He knew his initial silence had embarrassed her. He'd seen the pink flow to her cheeks and watched her downward gaze as she waited, but she hadn't held his awkwardness with words against him.

He wanted nothing but good to happen to this woman all the days of her life, and if what he'd seen so far was any sign, Amy getting to know Brady Maddox was going to be a great blessing, indeed.

CHAPTER 22

"Maybe I'd better start at the beginning," Brady said. "Instead of at the end."

"Please," Amy said. "I want to know everything."

"Want another soda?"

"I'm good, thanks."

"Where to begin?" he muttered.

"Let's start with how the two of you met."

"The first time I saw her, she was such a skinny, pitiful little thing." He closed his eyes, remembering. "All curled up in a corner of one of our stables. She'd run away from her foster family. There were problems developing between her and the mister, so she'd hightailed it out of there the first chance she got."

"I never knew she'd been raised in foster care," I said. "She's never talked about it."

"Darla always was closed-mouthed, so I'm not surprised, but she was a mess the day I discovered her laying there asleep, tangled hair down to her waist, dirty feet, and a torn gray dress that had been a hand-me-down from one of the other girls who lived at the foster home. Social services didn't pay a lot of attention to a foster teenager who ran away back then, so they never came looking for her, and we never contacted them. Darla was seventeen, close to aging out of the system anyway, so I guess she wasn't a priority."

"Still, they should have tried to find her," I said.

"And place her back in that home she had good reason to run from? No, it was best they didn't. She was the prettiest girl I'd ever met, even though she was plumb tuckered out that day, with dark circles under her eyes and hay caught up in her hair. She'd been hitch-hiking, trying to get as far away from that family as possible. A trucker had picked her up, but he made her get out of the truck in the middle of nowhere when he found out she wasn't interested in the same things he was interested in."

I couldn't imagine. My mother, only seventeen, hitchhiking along a highway with no place to go. The Desiree Stanton I knew always had some place to go and the money to get there.

"She had to walk a couple miles to get to our ranch. She said instead of risking hitchhiking again, she hid from the other cars and trucks that went by. Didn't want to take any more chances. Said she'd rather sleep in a ditch on the side of the road than climb back into another stranger's vehicle."

The idea of my mom as a teenager sleeping in a ditch alongside a road or curled up in some hay in a stranger's barn broke my heart. What had she endured that was so bad she'd felt forced to run away?

"Darla landed on her feet when she ended up at our place. At least, I thought she did. My mama took her in, of course. We gave her a job helping with the livestock."

"My mom helped with livestock?" Once again, I was shocked at what I was hearing. Desiree didn't even own a pet dog, cat, or canary and was vocal about never wanting to.

"She sure did. Your mom was a good worker," Brady said. "I was only nineteen, and I fell head over boots in love with her, of course. A lot of our ranch hands did. Darla could've had her pick of them. I was afraid I'd lose her if I didn't move fast, so the spring after she turned eighteen, we had ourselves a nice little wedding."

"So, what happened?" I asked. "When did things fall apart?"

"Well, I'd always been a good rider. Grew up in the saddle and had a knack for it, besides. I'd already won a few local competitions before Darla came along. After we got married, I felt invincible. I was a man with a beautiful young bride, and I wanted to be a good provider for her. Bull riding can win you a lot of money if you're good at it."

"And you were good at it?" I asked.

Instead of answering directly, he got up from the couch, lifted the cushion, dug around in the storage area beneath it, pulled something out wrapped in a soft cloth, and handed it to me. I pulled away the cloth and saw that it was a large, ornate, silver belt buckle, and it was heavy. There were words engraved on it: World Champion Bull Rider. I checked the date. It was the year before I was born.

"You won this?" I said with awe.

"I'll show you the picture," he said. "My sister kept a scrapbook for me over the years."

He pulled out a burgundy-colored scrapbook from beneath the same couch and flipped pages. He was searching for something in particular, so the pages flew by fast. I could see they were filled with clippings from his days on the rodeo circuit.

"Here you go." He handed it to me, opened to a clipping, and there in front of me was a dark-haired, young Desiree Stanton looking at Brady like he was her world. He had her tucked beneath one arm and was holding up the prize belt buckle with the other. They looked so happy standing there together I had to fight the tears. "What happened after that?" I handed back the scrapbook.

"When you get thrown off a bull enough times, it takes a toll. I was on the national rodeo circuit by then. Darla traveled with me. We had fun together, but there was almost always pain. I started eating Tylenol like candy. After a while Tylenol wasn't enough, and a buddy hooked me up with some stronger stuff. It took the pain away at first, like some sort of miracle, but after a while, it didn't work as well. I started drinking at night along with the pain meds to help me get to sleep."

"That was dangerous," I said.

"It sure was," Brady said. "But I was young and dumb. I lost my edge and got thrown off a bull named Red Tide. He was an evil thing. The meanest bull I've ever seen. If I believed in such things for animals, I would say he was demon possessed."

Brady closed his eyes against the memory.

"He threw me about three seconds into the ride, then he pranced all over me before the clowns could keep him from killing me. Two of them finally drew his attention for a few seconds while the third pulled me back behind the gate. Darla told me I was screaming so loud from the pain, everyone stopped talking and the place grew silent, and the only thing you could hear was my screams.

"Red Tide had done an awful lot of damage. My spine was broken and so were both of my arms and several ribs. I shouldn't have been moved, but Red Tide was acting so crazy, the other men thought they were doing the right thing by getting me out of there in a hurry."

I had never experienced enough pain to scream. Complain? Yes. Scream? No.

"How long were you in the hospital?"

"Nearly six months. Multiple surgeries, physical therapy, the works. This was back in '95—medical techniques weren't what they are today. I guess I looked pretty good to Darla when I was winning rodeo contests and piling up award money, but I didn't look so good after I got broke into pieces. The doctor told her he didn't think I'd ever walk again. After about three weeks of sitting beside me in the hospital, with tubes running in and out of me and monitors beeping, she cleaned out all the prize money sitting in our bank account and disappeared."

"Seriously?" I could hardly believe it—even out of Desiree. "I knew my mom could be selfish, but what a terrible thing to do!"

"It broke my heart. Not the money as much as the thought that she would do such a thing. I sold our trailer and moved back in with my folks after the doctors released me from the hospital. I spent the next two years in a wheelchair."

"Where did my mother go?"

"I don't know. None of us ever heard from her again."

CHAPTER 23

"**B**ut my mom is famous," I told him. "Her face has been on magazine covers. Didn't you notice her when she started starring in movies?"

"Ranchers don't spend a lot of time watching movies or thinking about movie stars. There's too much work and too few hands to do it. Hollywood? That's a different planet. It would never in a million years have occurred to me that Darla might end up on some movie screen."

"Didn't anyone else who knew the two of you make the connection?"

"Down through the years, a couple of people mentioned that there was an actress who reminded them of Darla. I was curious enough to watch one movie she was in, but it had been a lot of years, and the woman I saw wasn't the Darla I'd known. That actress looked different, talked different, and moved different. She even held herself different. Darla was beautiful, but she was sort of shy when she was young. I guess she must have gotten over it."

"Amy's mother is not shy now!" Lucas exclaimed.

Apparently, he was more traumatized by Mom than I'd realized.

"You must hate her for running out on you like she did and taking your prize money," I said. "You were the one who suffered the broken bones for it, not her."

"Sure. More than anyone I ever hated in my life," he said. "But I loved her, too. It would be hard not to. My hurt feelings aside, just imagine what that skinny little thing accomplished. She dolled herself up, pranced off to become a movie star, and actually succeeded. I'm impressed."

"And she was pregnant with me at the time," I said.

Brady nodded. "And she was pregnant with you."

I had such mixed emotions. What Brady said about her was true—what she had managed to do was amazing. That she did it as a young mother was even more so. The wonder of it to me was that she'd chosen to keep me with her instead of getting rid of me.

"She could have done a lot worse with her life," Brady said. "I was the one who ended up in prison, and she ended up famous. And somehow, she turned out a fine daughter at the same time." He shook his head in amazement.

"But she was a thief." It was hard for me to say those words. My mother had a lot of flaws, but to my knowledge, she'd never stolen anything.

"No, she wasn't. She was my wife. The money was in both of our names. Now that I know she was using the money to take care of our daughter, it's a lot easier to understand."

He was right. It might not have been ethical, but it was legal—unlike, apparently, her other four marriages. I'd save that thought for later. It was far too complicated to ponder now.

"I can't believe what I'm hearing," I said, my voice barely above a whisper. The portrait Brady painted of my mother was a shock, and yet there had always been something calculating beneath Desiree's charisma, a self-preservation instinct that overrode everything else.

"I'm sorry if that's hard to hear," Brady said gently.

"My whole life, I've watched her reinvent herself depending on what she needed or who she was with," I said, processing this new knowledge aloud. "New husband, new style, new friends. But this is different. This is…"

I couldn't finish the sentence. What word could capture the magnitude of abandoning an injured husband and taking his money?

"I don't know how to feel about her right now," I admitted. "I think I need time to process this."

Brady reached over and squeezed my hand. "You take all the time you need, sweetheart. Just don't let what happened between me and your mother poison what's between you and her."

"Don't you still hate her?" I asked.

"No." He shrugged. "Hate takes up too much energy, and I got tired of carrying it around. Plus, fear can make people do desperate things. Things they might never do under different circumstances. She was a nineteen-year-old kid who thought she was facing a lifetime of caring for a man who would never walk again. I wish she hadn't run, but I can understand why she did."

He shifted his weight and grimaced. "Could you pass me that bottle of Ibuprofen sitting over there on the sink?" He pointed. "The licks Furious Freddy gave me there at the end are kicking in now. They should never have put that kid on top of him. The boy was too green."

Lucas was closest to the sink. He grabbed the bottle and handed it to Brady.

Brady tossed a couple of tablets into his mouth, took a swig out of his can of soda, and swallowed.

"I've got a show in Pennsylvania tomorrow," he said. "I'll be there for a couple days and then I'll be headed back across Ohio to Chicago. I'm not sure what the schedule holds after that, but you and me will stay in touch and maybe we can spend some real time together after the rodeo season ends in the fall."

"I'd like that," I answered, thrilled that he wanted to get together again. "I'd like that a lot! How early are you heading out in the morning?"

"Oh, in about five hours."

I looked at my watch and was shocked at how quickly time had evaporated. "We've kept you up too long."

"Worth every blasted second," he said.

We exchanged contact numbers and addresses. Then, with nothing else left to do except leave, I looked at my father, and he looked at me. Then he opened his arms wide, and I walked into his embrace.

CHAPTER 24

After leaving the rodeo grounds, Lucas and I drove in silence for several miles. The emotional weight of meeting my father had left me both exhilarated and exhausted. I drove mechanically, my mind replaying every moment of our conversation.

"Are you hungry?" Lucas broke the silence. "I saw a sign saying there's a diner at the next exit."

I glanced at the clock on the dashboard. It was already past ten. "Do you think it's still open?"

"We can try it and see," he said.

The prospect of sitting in a diner, processing everything over a cup of coffee, sounded appealing. "Good idea."

The diner was indeed open, with a neon "Open 24 Hours!" sign buzzing above the entrance. Inside, a handful of customers sat scattered among the booths—a couple of truckers at the counter, an elderly couple sharing pie, and a solitary woman typing on a laptop.

We slid into a booth by the window. The vinyl seats squeaked beneath us. A waitress brought menus and took our drink orders— coffee for both of us.

"What are you thinking?" Lucas asked after the waitress left.

I traced the laminated edge of the menu with my fingertip. "Everything. Nothing. I'm still trying to believe it's real."

"I think your father is a good man."

"He is," I agreed. "Better than I dared hope." I set the menu aside. "Growing up, I invented so many versions of who my father might be. CIA agent, married politician, foreign prince…" I smiled at my childhood fantasies. "I never imagined a rodeo clown."

"Bullfighter," Lucas corrected, with a slight smile. "And a brave one."

The waitress returned with our drinks. Lucas ordered a slice of apple pie. I asked for more coffee.

"Did you notice," I asked after she left, "how he looked at me? Like he was memorizing my face?"

Lucas nodded. "He sees himself in you. There is a resemblance."

"You think so?"

"It's in the eyes and mouth. You tilt your head a little to one side when you are listening. So does he."

I wrapped my hands around the warm mug. "It's strange to see parts of myself reflected in a virtual stranger, but it makes me happy."

We fell silent as Lucas's pie arrived. I watched him eat methodically, his movements precise and deliberate.

"Do you think I should call my mom tonight and tell her I met him?"

Lucas considered this while chewing. "Would it bring peace or conflict?"

"Conflict, probably. At least at first." I sighed. "She worked so hard to keep this secret for so long, and I forced her to tell me."

"Then perhaps wait until you know your own heart better."

We lingered over coffee for nearly an hour; the conversation drifting between Brady, the rodeo, and simpler, everyday topics. By the time we left, I felt steadier, the emotional storm inside me settling into something more manageable.

Back in the car, we continued our journey home. The highway

stretched dark and empty before us, a black ribbon unspooling into the night.

"Your father is an interesting man," Lucas said. "Do you think he will come to visit you at the farm?"

"I hope so. Why?"

"I have been thinking about getting a bull," Lucas said. "I might hold off until he comes to visit. It would be valuable to have his knowledge beside me at the auction when I choose one."

"Why? Are you planning on riding it?"

"Of course not." He answered seriously, not picking up on the fact that I was teasing him. "Riding bulls can be dangerous."

"You think?"

Lucas ignored the sarcasm. "That was a lot for you to take in. Are you going to be okay?"

"Meeting my father was pure joy," I said. "What I'm struggling with now is how to feel about my mom. I'd like to say that I can't believe she would abandon a sick husband and steal his money, but Desiree is a selfish woman and has apparently been one for most of her life."

"Maybe she thought she had to be selfish to survive," Lucas said.

"Probably, but it still doesn't excuse her actions."

"Maybe. I cannot judge," Lucas said. "But the Bible says we are to honor our fathers and mothers. It does not say we are to honor them only if they deserve it."

"Do you think Desiree is worthy of honor?" I asked.

"She probably did the best she knew how."

I wasn't convinced, but it wasn't a topic I wanted to explore — at least not right then.

We drove several more miles in silence, both of us wrapped in our thoughts. Lucas stared out the window, seeing the same thing I was— a velvety dark sky with a moon so full and bright it seemed unreal. I couldn't remember ever feeling so happy.

That's when I made my mistake. "What are you thinking about so hard over there?"

I should have known better. Amish people tend to be honest to a fault, and I'd discovered that Lucas was even more honest than most.

"I am thinking it is time for me to find a wife."

I felt my heart thud. This was something I'd feared. I think he might have realized that. Perhaps he understood this topic would be painful for me.

"Not soon." His voice softened. "Marriage should not be entered in haste. But watching your father's joy in discovering he had a daughter reminded me I must find someone to marry if I am ever to have a child of my own. I have allowed my grief to blind me to that reality."

I grew nauseated at the mere thought of watching Lucas bring some new wife home to the *Daadi Haus* to start a family with. My mind went in a hundred directions at once, but my car went in only one direction—over the yellow line and into the oncoming lane. Lucas grabbed the wheel and jerked the car back into the right-hand lane.

"Careful!" Lucas said. "Let's not die tonight if we can help it."

He was right. I forced my attention back to staying safely in my lane. The thought of Lucas married to some other woman broke my heart, but I didn't want to kill both of us over it.

Unbidden, tears welled up. I had to blink hard to see well enough to drive. "Do you have anyone in mind?"

I know my voice quavered. By this time, I had met quite a few of the Amish women in his church. My neighbor, Erma, constantly had women coming and going in her home and she often asked me over for morning coffees. She had even invited me to come to help clean her house for church one Saturday. I thoroughly enjoyed the chattering and friendly teasing that went on between those who came to help. Many of those women were lovely, but most were already married. The two who were not married were closely related to him. Remembering that gave my heart a little relief.

"I do not have anyone in mind yet," he said. "But I do need to think about it."

"Absolutely." I forced my voice to remain steady.

"Do you ever think of having children?" he asked.

"I've wanted a bigger family my whole life," I said. "Of course I want children."

"Is there anyone back in your city home you might want to have children with?"

Oh gracious. Would the man not stop talking about children?

"Not so far," I said.

"That is good." He closed his eyes and tilted his seat back. "It is late. I must get up early, so I will sleep now."

Of course, he needed to sleep. It was just as well. The last thing I wanted was a long conversation about which Amish church settlements he should visit to find this new wife of his.

Lucas fell asleep almost immediately, his breathing deep and even.

CHAPTER 25

LUCAS

As Lucas leaned back, he felt relieved. It was out there now, in the open. He'd finally brought up the subject of finding a wife. Amy had to know it was a probability. Living a single life indefinitely did not feel like an option for him, and his attraction to Amy was becoming worrisome to him. In the beginning, after his sweet wife passed away, he was so stricken by grief it was hard for him to face even getting out of bed in the morning, let alone going about his work or even looking at another woman.

Three years later, here he was, sitting in Amy's car, trying not to look at her out of the corner of his eye, and wishing she had not worn such a short dress. The hem came down to her knees—modest by *Englisch* standards, but scandalous on an Amish woman.

As much as he would like to, he would not be doing either of them any favors by allowing them to grow any closer. It was best she knew the reality of his life and plans now. He knew his bishop was nervous for him because of the situation, but what was he supposed to do? Walk away from all the work he'd put into building up the farm? Dissolve the generous business agreement he and Amy had worked out? Plus, he really enjoyed living in the *Daadi Haus* that came with the job.

Then Amy briefly turned her head away, and quickly brushed tears from her eyes, as if hoping he wouldn't notice. But he did notice, and it broke his heart.

It wasn't his fault that Rick had made a decision that had shoved an intelligent, compassionate, lovable woman like Amy into his life. It wasn't her fault, either. If only...

No! He could not allow himself to even think about such a forbidden thing! Amy was off-limits and would remain so. That was all there was to it.

He closed his eyes and pretended to sleep, even though his heart and mind were aching.

CHAPTER 26

I was not surprised that Lucas fell asleep so soon, because I knew for a fact that he was usually up and working by four a.m.

I, however, was a mess. It seemed like the day had been endless, starting with my mother's surprise visit and ending with Lucas's pronouncement about finding someone to marry.

As I drove the dark roads with Lucas sleeping peacefully beside me, I wondered if he was dreaming about which lovely and competent Amish woman he should choose.

I shoved that painful thought into a mental drawer, slammed the drawer shut, double locked it, and began replaying every word my father had said tonight. I was thrilled that he was so happy to meet me, but I was deeply troubled by what he'd told me about Desiree. She had been young, of course. It was understandable why she wouldn't have looked forward to having an invalid husband for the rest of her life. Still, I didn't much like the person he had described.

I could now understand why she didn't want anyone to know who my father was after the way she had treated him. Bad publicity was usually better than no publicity at all for an actor—except in this case.

I could see a lot of her fans turning against her if they knew the entire story.

In less than a half-hour after leaving the diner, the adrenaline rush I'd felt over meeting my long-lost father drained away and I had trouble keeping my eyes open.

The rhythm of the road was hypnotic, the hum of tires on asphalt soothing. Without realizing how tired I'd become, I drifted off...

I was rudely awakened by several bone-shattering bumps and the sudden realization that I was sitting in the middle of a newly plowed field.

Lucas was already sitting straight up, wide awake, looking at me in disbelief.

I glanced around. The bumping of my car driving over freshly turned earth had jerked my foot off the accelerator, causing the car to come to a stop. We were alive, but there was no telling what might have happened to us had I fallen asleep at the wheel any place else.

"I'm so sorry! I'm so sorry!" The car engine had stopped. I tried to start it again, but my hands were shaking too hard.

I gave up on starting the car. I couldn't do it. My whole body was trembling too hard for fear of what might have happened. Then tears came.

Lucas unlocked my seatbelt. Then he came around to my side of the car, opened the door, and drew me out into his arms. He held me until the shaking and sobbing subsided.

"You are okay," he said. "We are both okay. There is nothing about this that cannot be fixed."

As comforting as it felt to be held by him, I tried to pull away. I did not want him to think that I was just some weak *Englisch* woman who needed to cling to him. I was already embarrassed enough by what I'd done.

He didn't allow me to pull completely away. Instead, in the bright moonlight, he bent his head down and gazed into my face. "Are you all right, Amy?"

"Yes," I said. "I am."

Some of my hair had tumbled over my left eye, and he gently pushed it aside. "The car is unhurt, we are unhurt. This is nothing to be worried about."

"But I could have gotten us killed," I said.

"You could have, but you did not," he said. "We will thank God for his deliverance and be more careful in the future. I am also at fault. I should have known you were too tired to drive, but I left you to drive alone. I blame myself."

What was I supposed to do with a man like this? A man who didn't curse at me for almost getting us killed, but who took the blame on himself, and treated me with kindness. I was so grateful to him for his understanding at that moment; it felt like my heart might burst.

If he had held onto me a second longer, I might have done something stupid, like kissing him from sheer gratitude. We were completely alone and far from prying eyes. I could feel the warmth of his fingers against the fabric of the back of my dress. I could smell the faint aroma of sandalwood still clinging to his skin.

He must have sensed what I was thinking, because he pulled away.

"Give me your car keys," he said. "I will drive the rest of the way."

That statement was such a shock, it brought me back to my senses.

"Excuse me?"

"You are in no shape to drive, and I am in no hurry to go to heaven." He reached out his hand. "May I have your car keys, please?"

"But..."

"Yes?"

I blurted out the first thing that came to my mind.

"But you're Amish."

"I am."

"Amish people don't drive."

He sighed, as though my ignorance depressed him.

"Most of us do not," he said patiently. "But some of us learn to drive during our *Rumspringa*—our running around time. Some of us

135

get driver's licenses and purchase cars just like anyone else. Then we sell the cars and start using buggies again after we join the church."

"You did that?"

"Yes."

"But if you drive my car tonight, you'd be driving illegally."

"I renew my driver's license every five years because I find it useful and less complicated to have it for identification," he said. "Owning a driver's license is not forbidden. It is owning a car that is forbidden. You are exhausted and still unsteady. I am rested and wide awake. If you trust me, I will drive us home."

"Won't your bishop be upset if he finds out?"

"Even our bishop would understand the necessity for caution after a driver has fallen asleep and driven into a field."

I decided if he wanted to break Amish protocol and drive us home, it would be a relief to let him do so.

I was a little surprised to find that I was still unsteady on my feet. I held onto the car to steady myself as I tucked myself into the passenger side. Then Lucas slid beneath the steering wheel, adjusted the seat, turned the keys in the ignition and before I knew what was happening, he'd expertly brought us out of the field and back up onto the road.

As he adjusted the rearview mirror, he chuckled.

"What's so funny?" I asked.

"People driving by here tomorrow are going to know what happened when they see the tracks of this car," he said. "And someday you and I will laugh about the night you fell asleep, and we both woke up in the middle of a stranger's field."

"Maybe someday," I said. "But not tonight."

"Not tonight. Get some rest," he said. "We will be home soon."

I didn't argue. I was too grateful to be alive. It was a pleasure to sit back and watch him deftly drive a car I had assumed would be a mystery to him.

"Do you enjoy driving?" I asked.

"Always," he said.

"What kind of car did you own?"

"A cherry red 1969 Pontiac GTO. I found it in pieces in a neighbor's barn when I was sixteen. I bartered work for it." He smiled at the memory. "It was in mint condition when I finished restoring it."

"A red GTO?" I laughed. "When you go on *Rumspringa*, you really go on *Rumspringa*, don't you?"

"It was something I wanted badly," he said. "My parents were embarrassed by it and made me park it behind our barn, but they did not fight with me over it."

"But you had to give it up?"

"I am Amish." He shrugged. "Giving up things we want is what we do."

I might have been mistaken, but I thought I detected a touch of bitterness in his voice.

CHAPTER 27

"Do you mind?" Lucas reached for the radio button.
This was another surprise. Once, when Erma was cleaning the house and I had Pandora on, Erma told me that her people weren't supposed to listen to the radio or any kind of popular music. I had turned it off out of respect for her church rules.

"Of course I don't mind, Lucas. Knock yourself out."

He fiddled with tuning it, going from station to station with the practiced movements of someone who had done this before. When he settled on a classical rock station playing "Hotel California," a small smile played at the corners of his mouth.

"I know I shouldn't," he said, noticing my surprise. "But just for tonight, perhaps God will understand."

For the remaining miles, I relaxed in the quiet cocoon of my car, while Lucas enjoyed getting to drive, and the comforting sounds of The Eagles played on my radio.

The drive ended way too soon for me, and I'm pretty sure Lucas wouldn't have minded a couple more hours on the road. When we arrived home, we both got out rather reluctantly, and Lucas dropped the keys into my hand.

"I am glad you found your father, Amy," he said. "Family is important. I am pleased that you invited me to go with you."

"Speaking of family," I said. "When do you think you will start searching for that Amish woman you plan to marry?"

"Not yet." In the light of a full moon, I could see him frown. "Courting someone will take more time than I can spare right now. There is Samuel still to be found, and I need to clean out the barn, spread manure, disc it in, plant the early vegetable crops, plus mend a couple fences, and prune all the fruit trees. I cannot begin my search until after those things have been accomplished."

I felt a rush of relief. At least there would be no new wife for me to deal with for a while.

"Do you like it here?" he asked, gazing up at the moon.

"Very much."

"You no longer miss the city?"

"I miss parts of it—like fresh bagels in the morning and half-price tickets to a Broadway show. But when I went back there last month to meet with the clients for this recent book, I missed being here more."

"Have you ever considered becoming Amish?" he asked, studying his boots.

"Why?" I laughed. "Are you planning on converting me?"

"That depends." He gave me a mischievous grin. "Do you need converting?"

"Probably," I said. "Why?"

He shrugged. "I just wondered if the thought has ever crossed your mind."

I carefully weighed my words. "I think I would really enjoy becoming part of such a close-knit community. But I couldn't do my job without electricity. I need Wi-Fi and a computer, and..."

"There is a library in town," he said, too quickly, as though he had already been thinking about it. "They have all those things. Some Amish use them."

"I know. But when I'm on deadline, I sometimes work all night long. Libraries don't keep those kinds of hours."

"When it comes to employment, our church is a little more lenient. There might be allowances made so that you could continue to work." He leaned against the side of the car. "It is not so hard being Amish once you get used to it."

What was he saying? Was this idle conversation or was he trying to tell me I would be in the running for his wife if I became Amish?

"I'm not sure I understand," I said. "Are you asking me to go to church with you?"

"No!" He sounded shocked I would suggest such a thing. "You should go with Erma or Gretchen."

"Let me get this straight—you are inviting me to church, but you don't want to be seen bringing me with you."

"Yes!" He seemed relieved that I understood.

"But we drive around together all the time."

"That is different."

"How is it different?"

"I just tell people you are my driver."

An *Englisch* man might have made up an excuse or even told a little white lie to spare my feelings. But Lucas? Not a chance. Have I mentioned that Amish men can be painfully honest?

"Perhaps you should buy a chauffeur's hat for me, Lucas," I said, hurt. "That would leave absolutely no doubt in anyone's mind about the status of our relationship."

He stared at me for a moment, as though trying to figure out what he'd said that upset me. Then he shook his head, turned and walked away.

CHAPTER 28

LUCAS

Lucas knew he'd made a mistake going to the rodeo with Amy. Driving her home had awakened longings he'd carefully buried years ago. The vibration of the engine, the responsive power beneath his hands, the open road stretching before him—these sensations had once been his greatest freedom. And that music—those forbidden melodies that had once filled his *Rumspringa* nights and days now played again in his mind, stirring memories he'd thought long surrendered.

That he'd asked her if she'd consider becoming Amish made him wince. What educated, independent woman would abandon her modern world for his? Why would Amy ever consider sacrificing her freedom in order to be with a man who split his days between field-work and barn chores, who came to dinner with callused hands he could never fully get clean, who had so little to offer her in material goods?

Remaining Amish was difficult even for him, and he had been raised in the church. It would be impossible for someone like Amy to understand.

And now he'd wounded her by admitting the truth—that to

protect both their reputations, he sometimes pretended she was merely his driver—not the woman who too-often filled his thoughts.

What Amy couldn't understand was the precarious position he occupied in his community. For an unmarried Amish man to live on the property of an unmarried *Englisch* woman created whispers, regardless of how separate their dwellings or innocent their relationship.

The arrangement made practical sense—the farm needed his constant attention—but in a world where perception often outweighed intention; he walked a narrow path.

His father understood such complexities. "The rules are there to serve our community, Lucas, not to punish us," he sometimes said while carefully navigating their bishop's expectations. "But God also gave us minds to think and hearts to feel compassion. Rules without thought become idols."

This wisdom was something Lucas held close, but rarely shared. Most in his community found security in their Ordnung's clear boundaries—precise measurements for dress hems, exact width for hat brims, specific colors and styles that set them apart from the world. These weren't arbitrary restrictions to Lucas but boundaries protecting a precious way of life centered on community rather than self.

He'd chosen this life with clear eyes, knowing both its beauty and limitations. He'd never openly defy their ways, but questions still lived in his heart—questions about grace and legalism, about where God's will truly lived.

How could he explain this complex religious dance to Amy? How could he make her understand that his feelings for her posed not just personal questions, but community and family ones?

So instead, he said nothing, and let the gulf between them widen.

CHAPTER 29

I lay in bed half the night, eyes wide open in the darkness, alternately savoring the wonder of meeting my father, and trying to figure out what on earth was going on in Lucas's head and if I should do anything about it.

I believed if I became Amish, Lucas might consider me potential wife material. If I did nothing, some unknown Amish woman would probably end up living in my *Daadi Haus*, married to a man I deeply admired.

Except for his restrictive religious culture, and a little social awkwardness, he was everything I had ever hoped for in a man and more, but his faith was part of the fabric of who he was. If he were to leave his church, would he even be the same person? I had no idea.

Did I love him? I was trying hard not to, but what woman in her right mind wouldn't fall for a man like Lucas?

Therefore, jumping through all the necessary hoops to become Amish was looking like something I should at least consider. It would involve eventually learning how to speak Pennsylvania Dutch, but I figured that was the least of my problems. Languages came easily to me. Learning how to milk a cow, give up my car, and wear a prayer *kapp* for the rest of my life wouldn't be easy, but for him, I could do it.

Living without electricity would be inconvenient, but I saw my Amish neighbors finding ways around it. Erma had a battery-operated floor lamp that worked so well she could see to quilt at night.

I enjoyed the coziness of using candles and kerosene lamps when the electricity had gone out for a few hours one evening back in the winter.

For a moment, I allowed myself to imagine us holding hands and gazing into one another's eyes, with the soft light of candles illuminating our happy faces.

I shook myself out of my fantasy. Lucas would put up with staring into my eyes for about thirty seconds before he'd feel the need to get up and put wood on the fire, check on the cattle, or fix something that was broken. The man didn't sit still for long unless he was reading, and then only after all the chores were done.

Thinking about the ramifications of making such an enormous life change kept me up half the night. About two o'clock, I remembered if we had children, they could only have an eighth-grade education. Could I live with that? Could they? What if, after joining the church, they decided it was too much and left? Would I be made to shun my own children? Would Lucas allow such a thing? The more I thought about it, the more complicated things became in my mind.

After a scant three hours of sleep, I crawled out of bed, showered, made coffee, and staggered to my desk. No matter what else was going on in my life, I had to keep to a regular writing schedule. The greatest danger a writer faced was letting the drama of one's own life eliminate the daily act of putting one word down on the page after another.

Coffee in hand, I stared at my desk for a moment, pondering the wisdom of staying here today. I didn't feel like I was up for talking to Lucas. With little sleep, I knew my filters would be down and there was no telling what I might say to him.

I decided it would be best if I just left for the day. My antique store beckoned as a sort of writing sanctuary where I could truly concentrate. If I needed a nap later, there were plenty of couches to choose from. The most important thing was that I wouldn't have the distraction of seeing Lucas every time I looked out a window.

CHAPTER 30

The antique store was quiet and still chilly, just like it had been the other day when Lucas and I had been here together. Instead of building a fire like he had, I turned the thermostat up, and found the office key behind the sales counter where I had seen Lucas replace it. I moved some of Rick's things out of the way, booted my laptop up, placed my notebook on the right side of his desk, and got straight to work.

The store had the perfect ambiance in which to write a historical memoir. I shoved all thoughts aside except for the story I was trying to capture.

It would have been lovely to open the blinds on the large storefront windows and let the spring sunshine in, but I'd done that once before and it was a mistake. Tourists and neighboring business owners had almost immediately begun tapping on the door, wanting to know if I was open. A "closed" sign was no deterrent.

So, surrounded by the peaceful company of vintage books and furniture, I sank into the world of the heroic World War II POW nurses who managed to provide health care under impossible and dangerous conditions.

Time stood still while I typed, which was always a sign that the writing was going well. The reality of our contemporary world evaporated as I heard the bombs blasting in the distance, felt the earth shake as I tried to concentrate on the wounded soldiers in my care, and felt the constant gnawing hunger from the starvation rations our captors gave us.

The words poured onto the page, and they were good words.

This—this was the reason I wrote. This hypnotic feeling of being in another time, another place. People hear about a runner's high, but there is a writer's high as well. The soaring feeling that comes when the story begins to tell itself, and our fingers fly, trying to keep up. Money was fine, but for most writers, it was this elusive charge of pure dopamine that we wrote for. I was a story addict, and finding the right words was my high. I continued to write feverishly, because I did not want this feeling to end.

I was utterly lost in the manuscript. Even thoughts of Lucas had disappeared, when I felt someone tap my shoulder. There was no reason for anyone to be in this building except me. I was so deep into my story, I jumped about a foot off the chair, screamed, and whirled around with an antique glass paperweight clutched in my hand.

The frightened Amish girl who had touched me was so surprised by my extreme startle reflex, she screamed back in terror.

"Goodness!" I said, my hand on my chest. My pulse was pounding.

"You left the back door unlocked," she said, once she calmed down.

"Which is something I won't do again!" My heart fell back into somewhat of a normal rhythm. "Is there something you wanted?"

"My *mamm* says you need someone to work for you?"

"And who is your mamm?"

"Erma's Betty."

"You're Erma's granddaughter?"

"Ja," she said. "I'm Betty's Prudence."

I'd run into this before. Amish people introducing themselves or being introduced by tacking on a relative's name. Erma was my neighbor and friend. Her daughter, Betty, had been one of the local people who had brought food after my ex-stepfather's funeral.

"How old are you, Prudence?"

"I'm seventeen."

She looked like she was about twelve, but that wasn't unusual. In pastel dresses and prayer *kapps*, no jewelry, no makeup, no tattoos, and no piercings, Amish teenage girls tended to look a lot younger than *Englisch* girls.

"You're looking for a job?" I asked. "What kind of job?"

"I am good at cleaning." She looked around at the hundreds of items displayed on the main floor. "It looks like you could use some help."

That was an understatement. I could use a lot of help with this place. The pseudo-Amish boy who had secretly lived here before I inherited it had been so bored, he had worked on cleaning and organized the main floor, but the second floor, which held literally tons of kitchen wares, hadn't been touched for months. Perhaps years.

"How much do you charge per hour, Prudence?"

"I don't know. Let me work here this afternoon and when I'm finished, you can pay me what you think I'm worth."

Smart girl. She had sized me up and knew if she did a good job, I'd end up paying her more than what she would be comfortable charging.

Amish young people were famed for their work ethic, and even in the Sugarcreek area, they were in short supply. If this worked out, I might even hire her to deal with customers when and if I opened the store up for business.

"Sure," I said. "Start on the second floor. Do whatever you think needs done." I pointed to a closet in the corner. "The cleaning supplies are in there."

Prudence marched upstairs with a mop under one arm, a bucket filled half-way with soapy water in one hand, several dusting cloths tucked into her apron pocket, and a small stepladder under the other arm. I went back to my writing. I had almost gotten back into the story when I heard a crash directly over my head and a yelp. I ran upstairs and found Prudence sitting on the floor with a dusting cloth in one hand, and her right leg through a stepladder. I helped her untangle herself—she wasn't particularly hurt and was very apologetic —and then I went back downstairs to continue working.

A half-hour later, I felt a drop of water fall on my head. Again, I ran upstairs.

"What's going on?" I asked, although I was fairly certain where the water had come from when I saw Prudence mopping the floor with copious amounts of water. "There's water dripping from the ceiling."

"I need to get this floor clean!" There were tears in her eyes, which I ignored.

"No," I said. "You don't. You don't have to do anything at all. It was you who came asking for a job from me, remember? I don't want mop water dripping on me or my computer. Why don't you stick with dusting?"

"Okay."

Crisis averted, I went back to my typing.

I had almost completed two pages before I heard crying upstairs. This time I didn't run. I plodded up the stairs, dreading what I would find next. What I found was Prudence huddled on the floor in a corner, crying her eyes out. I glanced around, expecting to find some crisis like a broken window, but nothing seemed to be amiss except an Amish girl sobbing.

CHAPTER 31

I am not without compassion. I shoved all thoughts of the book I was trying to write aside to go sit on the floor with this obviously distraught girl. I put my arm around her, and she leaned into me.

"Do you want to tell me what's wrong?" I asked.

She shook her head. Curled up like she was, her apron didn't completely cover her belly, and her dress was drawn tightly over it. I considered keeping quiet, but sometimes something has to be said.

"Are you pregnant, Prudence?"

She gasped, sat straight up, and covered her abdomen. "You can tell?"

"Is that why you're crying?"

She sniffled. "Yes."

"Is marriage to the boy a possibility?"

She shook her head.

"Have you told your family?"

"No." At the mere thought of telling her family, she wailed. "My *daett* is going to kill me."

I'd met her dad when he and Betty had brought food over. He was a slender man with a ready smile and compassionate eyes. I doubted he had any intention of killing anyone, least of all his daughter.

"Are you in love with the baby's daddy?"

"Yes."

"Does he know about the baby?"

"Not yet."

"Is he Amish?"

She shook her head again.

Well, that certainly complicated things. This was much more than I knew how to handle. I had no idea how the family dynamics of an Amish family worked if a girl got pregnant and marriage wasn't an option. Did they kick her out? Shun her? Give the baby up for adoption? I needed Lucas. He would know what to do.

"I think you've done enough work for one day," I said. "Why don't you go on home?"

"Please don't tell my family."

"Of course not," I said. "You will have to do that, yourself."

Reluctantly, she got up off the floor, and I did, too.

"Do I have the job?"

"No," I said. "At least not yet. You have some really heavy decisions to make, and I suggest you talk to your parents sooner rather than later. If you still want a job later, when you get things figured out, I'll be here."

After the poor girl left, my phone dinged, and I saw my father had texted with a date for next month, when he'd be performing at the Buckin' Buckeye again. I couldn't wait.

I wondered what he'd think of this place. Maybe I could ask his advice on what to do with it. The idea of having a dad to go to for advice made me feel a little giddy.

If he came to see it, I'd enjoy showing him this desk and telling him the story about my secret drawer and the confederate money I discovered in it.

Speaking of which, although I knew there would be nothing in the hidden drawer now, I was curious to see if I could find it again.

With my writing session already interrupted, I crowded into my childhood hidey hole, and there it was—the drawer I'd discovered so many years ago. I opened it, not expecting to find anything, but it was far from empty.

CHAPTER 32

I nside the hidden drawer were three pages of careful handwriting on creamy, high-quality paper. I was thrilled to discover that it was a letter from Rick to me.

He had written it with an old-fashioned fountain pen, and a memory rose from the depths of my consciousness—Rick showing me how to draw ink from a jar into a fountain pen by using a tiny lever. As a child, the process was fascinating.

The beginning of the letter was a pleasant surprise. That he was clever enough to think I would remember and look for the drawer pleased me.

I smiled when I read his explanation about planting the Confederate money and other items in the drawer to give me a history lesson. There was no doubt in my mind that it had helped create a love of history within me, for which I was grateful.

I sat on the floor and settled back against the desk with the letter in my hands, looking forward to reading the rest of what he had to say.

Then the letter took a surprising turn.

I tried hard to be a good step-father to you—for the few years your mother allowed it.

What you don't know is how deeply I regret not fighting harder for you when Desiree and I divorced. I've carried that regret for years. She had leverage over me I allowed her to use, and I've never forgiven myself for letting you go so easily.

During my time at Sotheby's, I made some poor choices. I took a few items that spoke to me. It wasn't about money; it was about possessing beauty I couldn't otherwise afford. Your mother discovered this, and when we were going through our divorce, she said if I contested custody or pushed for visitation rights, she would expose everything.

I chose my freedom and reputation over fighting for you, but I've never fully forgiven myself—or her—for allowing you to be used as a bargaining chip in our separation.

After our divorce, I became obsessed with curiosity about your mother's past. She had shared nothing with me about her childhood or where she grew up. During our marriage, I'd noticed her strange reactions the few times anything Amish was mentioned. She was always uncomfortable the few times we were around them. She also had peculiar knowledge no one would ever expect. For instance, she was an excellent traditional cook when we were alone. Sometimes she would do needlework privately when she was stressed, skills she hid from her friends.

I was so focused on finding out Desiree's secrets, that I eventually hired a private investigator. It took a long time, but he eventually traced her to the Schlabach family in Sugarcreek. Born to an ultra-strict Amish family, she ran away at seventeen.

I came to Sugarcreek seeking answers, not revenge. When I

discovered her childhood home was for sale, I purchased it because I felt you deserved to know your heritage someday. The farm is more than just a place to live; it is a connection to the roots Desiree hid from you. What you do with it is up to you.

By now, you might have already learned about your biological father, Brady Maddox. The name Darla Sanders, which is what Desiree gave him, was a complete fabrication. From what I understand, she was in terrible shape when she showed up at the Maddox's. I do not know how she got to their ranch, but it's a long way between Ohio and Texas.

Your mother's birth name was Dorcas Schlabach. A solid Amish name and one I'm certain she hated. Her parents, Amos and Hazel Schlabach, never heard from her again once she left. She was their only child, born when they were well into their late forties.

From what I understand, Amos was a strict disciplinarian, and young Dorcas had a wild streak. His attempts to force her into being an obedient Amish girl had the exact opposite effect. She became a legend in the Amish community as she rebelled.

Fortunately, the work ethic she had been forced to develop left her in good stead once she became an actress. She always had a reputation for working harder than anyone else on set.

I've never threatened Desiree with revealing her true identity, nor have I contacted her about the farm. I simply restored it, lived in it, and now I'm passing it to you—your rightful inheritance. I had to have it gutted when I first moved in. The entire place needed to be wired for electricity, of course, and plumbing. Desiree's parents were from one of the strictest Amish sects and didn't allow indoor plumbing, comfortable furniture, or much of anything else.

Knowing all this has helped me forgive Desiree for much of the pain she's created. As the old saying goes, "Hurt people hurt people."

So now, you know everything. This knowledge will probably complicate your relationship with your mother, but I believe you deserve the truth and I'm not sure she would ever tell you otherwise. There's an entire history here in Sugarcreek that belongs to you.

One more thing—attached to this letter is a list, along with who to contact to return the items I took from Sotheby's, and where each item is kept. You can use this letter—written in my own hand—as my confession and apology. You weren't even born when they were stolen, so no one can accuse you of wrongdoing. I need to make this right, even if I'm not here to face the consequences.

Enjoy the farm and the store. Treat Lucas Hershberger well if he stays on. Thank you for being part of the best years of my life, and good luck with your mom.

Love,
Your stepdad, Rick

I don't know how long I sat, trying to wrap my mind around what I'd just read. Rick's letter was too much to take in all at once. I found it hard to reconcile the man I thought I knew with the one I'd just met in the letter. I was equally stunned to find out the truth about my mother's background.

How had she done it? Marriages required birth certificates. I knew there were illegal ways to get one, but was Desiree smart enough to pull it off? I barely gave it a moment's thought. Of course she was.

I glanced at the attached list of things he'd stolen. A couple of paintings by artists I didn't know, some Faberge miniature animals, a Tiffany clock. I would have to find and return every item. So much trauma and guilt for things that had become a burden to him in the end.

And apparently, Desiree was an even better actress than I knew. She hadn't lifted an eyebrow in surprise when she came to see my new home. I felt a grudging respect for my mother's cool actions. The only possible giveaway I could remember was not wanting to stay for more than a few minutes each time she'd visited.

CHAPTER 33

I couldn't settle down. I attempted, but it was useless. Too much had happened. I couldn't concentrate. My mind was heavy with questions about my mother, and her life here. I had no desire to write any more today.

In fact, I had no real desire to do anything except go home, crawl into bed, and pull the covers over my head and sleep until things made sense.

Then something occurred to me. Erma was a few years older than my mother. As neighbors, they would have known one another.

Without waiting another moment, I locked up and went out to the car. Fifteen minutes later, I let myself into the back door at Erma's farmhouse and found her working in her kitchen.

"Welcome!" Erma said. "Is it not a lovely spring day?"

It really was, but I'd been way too immersed in my thoughts to pay attention.

She was standing at her kitchen table, her hands busy kneading dough for cinnamon rolls. She did this every Friday. All of her grown children and grandchildren lived nearby and were in the habit of stopping by on Friday evenings to get one of her famous giant rolls and to have a chat. Even those grandchildren of hers who were on *Rumspringa* would stop by before going on to whatever party or event they had planned.

"Good food brings a family together," she told me once. "I do not allow more than a week to go by without knowing how my children and grandchildren are doing. My cinnamon rolls draw them to my door and make it unnecessary to hitch my old horse up to the buggy."

As Erma dove into kneading that massive ball of dough. I made note of the fact that although she had to be past sixty, her arms were still strong and muscular. I suspected kneading this dough every week might have something to do with it.

"Can I help?"

I had tasted Erma's pastries. I could easily understand why her entire family made time to drop by when she had baked.

"Sure!" Erma glanced at the clock. "I am a little behind. I'll get you an apron while you wash your hands."

Shaping the bread dough into cinnamon rolls felt lovely, especially after Erma tied an apron around my waist and handed me a rolling pin and knife. The dough was warm and yielding beneath my fingers, releasing the heady scent of yeast and cinnamon as I worked. Her family was so large, she always made two big commercial sized pans of her rolls.

As we worked together, my fingers sinking into the soft dough, I thought about how to get answers without giving away the reason behind my questions. If Erma knew why I wanted to know about the Schlabachs, she could not keep that knowledge to herself. The kitchen was filled with morning light streaming through the window, high-lighting the dust motes that danced in the air.

I rolled the dough out, cut it into strips and formed the rolls like I'd seen Erma do. The familiar motions were soothing, giving me courage to ask casually, "I've been wondering about the history of my house. Did you know the people who lived there before Rick?"

"The Masts? I knew them well." Erma's hands never stopped

moving as she spoke, her fingers deftly shaping perfect spirals. "They lived there about five years. Good people. Seven children. The oldest boy married an Amish girl from out west—somebody he'd met through friends—and after the wedding, she was miserable living here. Missed her family and cried all the time. Tom Mast tired of having an unhappy daughter-in-law, so he packed up his family and moved to Colorado where her people were."

"Did it work out?"

"Tom's wife, Martha, didn't care for Colorado—and was upset with Tom for making them leave, but she has ten grandbabies out there now and her other children have settled nearby, so she's fine. She's a scribe for The Budget now and I always enjoy looking for her letters about what's going on in their church and family."

"That's who Rick bought the farm from?"

"Yes, but it sat empty for a while. The Masts were asking too much at first. The house was empty nearly a year before Rick came along."

"Who else lived there before the Masts?"

"That would be the Kauffmans. Older couple. He hurt his back falling out of a deer stand, and they had to move in with their daughter over in Wooster."

"A deer stand?" I said, surprised. "He was hunting?"

"Of course," Erma said. "Venison is good meat."

"But I thought the Amish didn't own guns."

"Of course we do—but he was bow hunting, and was too excited climbing into his stand to tether himself."

I digested this bit of information before asking, "So who lived here before the Kauffmans."

Erma made a face like she'd just tasted something bitter. "That would be the Schlabachs."

"What were they like?" I kept my eyes on my own less-perfect rolls.

Erma's rhythm faltered slightly. "They weren't part of my church. They went to a much stricter one."

"How strict?" I tried to match her efficient pace, but it was impossible.

"Very." Erma's lips pressed into a thin line as she dumped some powdered sugar into a bowl, added vanilla, and whipped hot water into it with quick, practiced strokes. "Amos Schlabach was a man who had soured on life, and no one knew why. When his wife got pregnant at age forty-six and delivered their one and only child, everyone thought he'd be happy—but it didn't turn out that way."

"Why?" I watched her capable hands whisk the icing to a smooth consistency.

"I don't know. Some said he'd wanted a boy so badly, he couldn't love the girl he got. Little Dorcas was a sweet baby and toddler, but Amos took that old saying, 'spare the rod, spoil the child' to heart. It seemed like that child could do nothing right."

"In what way?"

"Well, one day, I think she was about seven, he caught her out in the woods, standing on the stump of a tree he'd cut down. She was singing a song she'd made up, like children do, and she was pretending she was singing to an audience. It was so innocent. She had such a pretty little voice. When that old man saw her doing it, he punished her. Can you imagine?"

My hands stilled on the dough. "What about her mother?"

"Hazel?" Erma set down her whisk and wiped her hands on a kitchen towel, leaving ghostly white fingerprints of flour. "She was the kind of woman who thought her husband's will and decisions were law. I never saw her stand up for Dorcas, and I was there at their house a lot because she was a sickly woman and needed help with the housework."

A bird called outside the window, its cheerful sound at odds with the story unfolding in the warm kitchen.

"My mother made me and my sisters take turns going over and helping until Dorcas was old enough to take over." Erma's voice grew softer as she arranged the rolls in the pans. "That girl worked so hard.

Her mother needed her in the house, and with no sons to help carry the burden, Amos needed her in the fields. I remember seeing her hands when she was a teenager, and they were as calloused and rough as a man's."

I thought about Desiree's daily hand cream routine. She had beautiful hands now, and I was glad for her. The contrast between the hardworking Amish girl and my glamorous mother made my heart hurt.

"So, what finally happened to Dorcas?" I asked, trying to keep my voice steady as I placed the last roll in the pan. I didn't want Erma to know how hungry I was for anything she could tell me.

Erma covered the pans with clean kitchen towels. "The child waited until she was seventeen before she ran away. My sister said she was surprised Dorcas waited that long." Her eyes grew distant, looking beyond the kitchen walls to a past only she could see. "We heard later that somebody had seen her getting into the cab of an eighteen-wheeler at a truck stop out on the Interstate. No one ever saw her or heard from her again, as far as I know."

Erma leaned against the counter, absently brushing flour from her apron. "I've always wondered how her life turned out. I can't imagine how she supported herself. She didn't have any kind of ID—not even a birth certificate—and no money that anyone knew about."

"Why didn't she have a birth certificate?" I asked, my pulse pounding as pieces of a long-hidden puzzle fell into place.

"The people in their church believed in allowing the government to have as little say in their lives as possible." Erma moved to the sink and began washing her hands, the water running loud in the quiet kitchen. "Many had home births and didn't bother registering any of their children."

"Didn't they ever get the police involved to find her?" I joined her at the sink.

"I can't imagine Amos reporting it." Erma handed me a clean towel. "Her mom died a few months after Dorcas left. Amos sold the house and moved up to Mt. Hope. I think he passed on, too, a few years later."

The cinnamon rolls were finished, lined up in neat rows beneath their towel coverings. All they needed now was to rise again, get baked, iced, and Erma would be all ready for her family to come by for their weekly dose of her love and wisdom. The sweet, spicy scent of cinnamon filled the kitchen, but I barely noticed it now.

"I'd better go," I said, untying the apron with fingers that trembled slightly.

"Thanks for the help," Erma said, taking the apron and hanging it on a wooden peg by the door.

"Any time," I said, my mind already racing with the bleak picture Erma had painted of my mother's childhood.

As I drove home from Erma's, the pieces of my mother's life—her real life, not the fabricated Hollywood version—were finally falling into place.

"Dorcas Schlabach." I said it out loud. The name felt foreign to my tongue, yet it explained so much.

A wave of emotions washed over me—anger at Mom's deceptions, empathy for the trapped girl she once was, awe at the sheer force of will it must have taken to transform herself so completely. I gripped the steering wheel tighter as I navigated a curve in the road. I remembered how she'd shivered when talking about the Amish. That hadn't been disdain—it had been fear. Possibly fear of being pulled back into a world she'd fought to escape.

I couldn't condone what she'd done to Brady, or her lifelong web of lies. But for the first time, I felt I could begin to understand her. The girl who had fled an oppressive father, who had reinvented herself through sheer will power—that girl was still somewhere deep inside my glamorous, talented, difficult mother.

Knowing her story didn't excuse her behavior, but it gave it context. I noted the fact that she'd kept the same initials. Desiree Stanton. Darla Sanders. Dorcas Schlabach. A clever touch from a woman who had made an art of reinvention.

Now, the question was, what would I do with this information? The afternoon sun slanted through the trees as I approached my farmhouse, casting dappled shadows across the windshield. Would I tell her what I knew? If I did, would it make us closer, or cause us to drift further apart? With Desiree, you never knew.

CHAPTER 34

W hen I got home from Erma's, Lucas was sitting on the back steps, whittling on a stick.

"Someone brought you flowers." He jerked his thumb back over his shoulder. "They are on the kitchen table."

"Flowers? For me?"

"Well, they are not for me." He sounded grouchy, which was unusual.

I'd seldom received flowers from anyone. I rushed into the kitchen and saw a lovely blue flower-sprigged teapot filled with a dozen delicate pink rosebuds and white baby's breath. There was a small, sealed envelope with my name on it. I pulled it from the holder and opened it.

"If I had been around when you were a little girl, this is something I'd have bought for you. Happy first day of being father and daughter! Love, Brady."

I carried the note out onto the porch to show Lucas. "It's from Brady!"

Lucas read it. Then he handed it back and picked up his knife again.

"I did not know it was from your father. I thought it might be from some man friend back in New York City."

"Nope," I said. "No secret admirers for me."

He seemed strangely somber and withdrawn. I decided I'd wait until he was in a better mood to bring up Rick's letter.

"Where have you been?"

"Erma's."

He nodded. "Was she making her cinnamon rolls?"

"As always on a Friday afternoon. Where did you go?"

"I went over to TMK Farm Service to pick up more chicken feed. We were almost out. Their baby chicks were in, so I bought three for the girls."

"I bet they were thrilled."

"Sure were. The chicks already have names."

"How is everyone over there?"

"Gretchen received another money order from Samuel." He closed his whittling knife with a snap and brushed the wooden curls into the flower bed.

"Was there a note?"

"Nope. The money order came from Erie, Pennsylvania."

"Is that significant?"

"I think it might be. Before he married Gretchen, Samuel went to stay with an *Englisch* uncle who lived in Erie. I'm going to try to get in touch with the uncle."

"And then what?"

"It's only a three-hour drive to Erie. I was hoping you'd take me there when I find out something."

"I'll be happy to," I said. "But isn't going to see him a job better left to Samuel's brothers?"

"Perhaps," Lucas said. "But I am eager to have a private talk with my brother-in-law. I want to be the one who tells him face-to-face that his three little girls cry for him every night."

CHAPTER 35

W hat Erma had told me about my mother gave me yet another restless night. The life Desiree lived now was such a far cry from the life she'd experienced in this very house as a child.

I wanted to find out more. What had her life been like as a child besides what sounded like endless work?

I hoped Erma wouldn't get sick of me, but I needed to pay her another visit. I put in several morning hours on the book I was writing, then after lunch, I took a small basket and went outside to the large strawberry patch Lucas had nurtured into some of the sweetest berries I'd ever tasted. One restaurant in town had an order in for everything Lucas could bring them. I hoped he wouldn't mind if I took a few to Erma.

When I arrived, she was outside with a paint brush refreshing the white on the banister of her front porch.

"That looks nice, Erma."

Her hair was tied in a kerchief, and she was wearing what appeared to be her oldest dress. It was light blue, worked stained, and now covered in white paint splatters. Erma was not a neat painter.

She'd managed to get paint on her face, hands, arms and kerchief, too, but the smile she gave me was bright with welcome.

"What have you got there?" She waved at me with a paintbrush that looked so bedraggled, I felt sorry for it. "Are those Lucas's strawberries? Those things are like gold around here."

She laid her paintbrush on the paint can lid, and I handed her the basket. She rinsed it with water from her garden hose. She ate a strawberry, then offered me one. I shook my head.

"These really hit the spot!" She said, consuming another one.

"I thought you'd enjoy them. I also thought you'd like to know that we've had word about Samuel."

She wiped strawberry juice from her fingers onto the skirt of her already soiled work dress. "Is he okay?"

I told her about the money order from Erie.

"Well, at least we know he's alive." She selected another strawberry. "I keep thinking he'll come back on his own soon. It's hard for Amish men to be away from their families for very long. They get homesick too easily."

"They do?"

"Not sure all of them would admit it, but most of them are total homebodies. My husband hated being away from us so much, he gave up the good-paying job he had with an *Englisch* carpentry crew, and taught himself how to repair shoes so he could stay home."

"He could make enough money to support your family by repairing shoes?"

"Of course not," Erma said. "So, I began cleaning other people's houses. Our older children got jobs and helped as well. We were fine. We all felt that it was worth everything we could do to have *Daett* home with us."

The image she painted of a family pulling together to keep the father at home was a poignant one. It reminded me of why I had come to see her.

Lucas's question the night before about if I'd ever thought about

174

becoming Amish, combined with my new knowledge of my mother's childhood, had created a strong curiosity within me. Apparently, I came from a long line of Amish people. My mother had rejected it, but that didn't mean I had to.

I had grown up without knowledge of any family except my mother. Now, I was being presented with knowledge of roots that went so deep I could hardly imagine all the family and connections I might have. I wanted to know what it felt like to be truly Amish.

"Would your church allow me to come to church services?"

She hopped off the porch and picked up the paintbrush again. "It is not forbidden."

"Do you mind if I go with you tomorrow?"

"Why would you want to?" Erma gave me a penetrating look. "You won't enjoy it. The service goes on for a very long time and you will not understand a word. Our worship is not designed for outsiders to watch. We are not an evangelistic people."

I hesitated. I didn't want to talk about my mother yet, and I certainly didn't intend to risk letting her know about my feelings for Lucas. Erma was a loyal friend, but I wasn't naïve enough to trust her with a confidence.

"I would like to know more about the Amish," I said. "I have a great respect for your people. I thought going to church with you would help me understand and learn more."

"I think I've done as much painting as I want to do today," she said. "Why don't we go into the kitchen? You can help yourself to a cup of coffee while I wash up. Then we'll talk."

A blue enamelware coffee pot always sat on the back of Erma's wood stove, perpetually filled with a strong black brew. I'd had her coffee twice before. One cup and I stayed up half the night writing page after page before I crashed. That experience had taught me part of the secret behind Erma's prodigious productivity.

"I'd really appreciate that."

I needed to write at least five thousand words before the day was over to hit my quota for the week, and after my virtually sleepless night, Erma's coffee would help.

She put the lid back on the paint can, pounded it in place with the handle of the paintbrush. There was a trash can on her back porch, and she dropped the paintbrush in it as she passed by.

"Don't tell anyone you saw me do that," she said. "But I hate cleaning paint brushes, so I buy cheap ones and throw them away when I'm finished."

"I won't tell."

After cleaning the paint off her hands and pouring both of us cups of her liquid jet fuel masquerading as coffee—she sat down across from me at the table and folded her hands.

"Sometimes *Englisch* people come to this area, and they fall in love with what they see as a simpler way of life. Sometimes they think they want to become Amish themselves. Is that why you are asking to attend church services?"

"I've considered it," I said.

"That's what I was afraid of," Erma said. "Becoming Amish is more than just wearing long dresses, riding in buggies, and milking cows. That is just the surface stuff, Amy. It involves so much more than that."

"Like what?"

Erma rose, went to her refrigerator, and pulled out a plate with four cinnamon rolls on it.

"I can't believe you had leftovers," I said. "Didn't all your family come?"

"Jim and Helen and their two youngest are at a wedding in Pennsylvania this week."

She put one of the tasty treats on a flowered plate and handed it to me without bothering to ask if I wanted it. Fortunately, I did. Then she sat back down and served herself one.

"I really shouldn't," she said. "But I hate to see good food go to waste."

176

"I agree," I said. "Now, tell me more about what it's like to become Amish. Not that I'm planning on it. I just want to know what you think."

"Being obedient to all our church's rules can be very difficult. That would be very hard for you, I think. Along with the willingness to sacrifice so many things *Englisch* people take for granted."

I took a big bite of cinnamon roll. It was like biting into a taste of cinnamon scented heaven. "I'd still like to go to church with you."

"I can count the *Englisch* people I've known who successfully converted to the Amish way of life, on one hand with fingers left over, Amy."

If she was trying to discourage me, she was succeeding. I was just stubborn enough to push it with her, though. Maybe becoming Amish wasn't for the faint of heart, but I didn't want to give up that easily. I could at least think about it.

"We have had visitors before, but they rarely come back for a second visit. If you come with me tomorrow and you will know why. Our services will be especially long tomorrow. We will select a new minister from five candidates. Also, the bishop will tell the people about Prudence's situation."

"Prudence's situation? Your granddaughter Prudence?"

Erma lowered her eyes. "My granddaughter has confessed to us and to the bishop that she is four months pregnant with an *Englisch* boy's baby. The father lives in Millersburg, and she says he lost interest in her as soon as he found out that she was with child."

"Oh!" I pretended to know nothing. "And how is everyone taking it?"

"Her parents are not happy with her," Erma said. "Nor am I. She has been a very foolish girl."

"What happens to an Amish girl if she gets pregnant and isn't married?" I asked.

"If it is with an Amish boy, there is usually a hurry-up wedding with fewer guests than usual," Erma said. "If it is an *Englisch* boy, things get more complicated. It will not be pleasant for any of us, but ultimately, we will deal with it and the baby will be loved."

"So, Prudence won't be shunned?"

"Not now that she's confessed her pregnancy and asked for forgiveness."

I went to the sink to wash the sweet stickiness from the cinnamon rolls off my fingers. "Somehow, I assumed there would be a harsher punishment."

"My people have never pretended to be anything but human, Amy. We struggle with sin, too." Erma automatically rose to pull a clean dish towel out of a drawer for me to dry my hands. It had been line-dried and smelled of spring sunshine. Then Erma sat back down. Her thoughts were so focused on Prudence, I doubted she even realized she'd gotten up.

"We understand human frailty well—especially that of a young girl who believed the love words she heard coming out of the mouth of an *Englisch* boy. There will be tears, but Prudence will not be cast aside. We will continue to love and care for her and the baby, but our Prudence will have to grow up quickly now."

"Is there anything I can do for her?" I folded the dish towel and placed it on the counter.

"For Prudence? Purchase a baby gift if you wish. That's about it."

We sat in silence, grown women grieving the hurt we knew Prudence would have to go through.

Then Erma gave a great sigh. "There are still two cinnamon rolls left. I think they'd go good with a second cup of coffee right about now. Want one?"

Did I want more sugar and cinnamon? After this conversation?

"Absolutely!"

CHAPTER 36

The next morning, I dressed in a plain black skirt, a black top, along with a black sweater, black tights, and black shoes. I'd seen a few Amish people walking to church, and I thought I would blend in better this way. I also put my hair up in a plain twist and covered it with a small, black headscarf because I knew head coverings were important to them—although I wasn't sure why or if the scarf would be enough. I also wore no makeup or jewelry.

I reconsidered once I was completely dressed and took a long look at myself in the mirror. Black is not a good color for me. It felt like I was going to a funeral instead of a church. The shock of seeing myself dressed like that caused me to take everything off and search through my closet for something else to wear—something plain but with a little color—except there wasn't anything else that was appropriate. Resigned, I put my black ensemble on again.

Women will do nearly anything for the man they might love, including dressing like an eighty-year-old Italian grandmother.

Instead of riding in Erma's buggy, I picked her up in my car, which she had requested.

"It'll save me hitching up the buggy," she'd said. "The house where we are worshipping today is only three miles away. It doesn't seem worth getting poor old Tommy all hot and lathered up. He's getting old and grumbles when he has to leave the farm."

"Not a problem, Erma," I'd said.

Erma loaded two fresh pies into the back of my SUV. "These are for the lunch we'll have later."

"Should I have brought something?" I asked.

"No," Erma said. "You are a guest. But if you become one of us, you will be expected to bring food each church Sunday and host church once a year."

"How many people go to your church?" I asked.

"About forty families."

I couldn't envision what forty families would look like. "But how many people?"

Erma looked confused. "I don't know. We just always count families."

"But why?"

"I guess it's because individualism is not encouraged within the Amish community," she said. "We are more interested in how many families we have. We are growing so quickly, we are at a point that we may need to start a new church!"

Because I'd had that last-minute loss of confidence over my dress, we were a little late. Not much. But with needing to park in the field across from the house and then walk across the field and up the steep driveway, we were the last ones to enter the barn.

They were singing as we entered. It's hard to describe, but it was like no singing I'd ever heard. I did not recognize the tune, of course, which was slow and sounded like a drone with male voices taking precedence. The seats were a combination of rows of backless benches and bales of hay lining the walls of the barn. I wondered at the uncomfortable seating choices when many of the men were so capable of making fine furniture.

The men sat on one side and the women sat on the other. The two groups faced each other with an open space in the middle for the speaker.

Erma and I found an open spot on a bench amid the women's side and got settled in for what I had been warned would be a very long worship service. Once they stopped singing, one man stood up and began speaking in Pennsylvania Dutch.

Instead of paying attention to words I couldn't understand, I watched the little children wander back and forth between their parents or grandparents. They would be welcomed into various dad or grandfather's arms, and then, when the child grew bored, they would wander back to their mothers and grandmothers.

Some children ran to the back of the barn to get a drink of water from a large yellow cooler. Some ran outside the barn, presumably to use the toilet. Children being what they are, I wondered at the time they stayed gone. I suspected a bit of playtime stolen. The parents didn't seem to be bothered by it.

Several of the mothers had brought homey toys to keep their smallest children occupied. One little girl carefully folded and unfolded her mother's pretty handkerchief. It didn't seem like much of a toy to me, but she seemed content. A little boy ran a tiny toy tractor across his grandfather's large Bible.

This wasn't so bad. While I was thinking I would be willing to do this every other Sunday for Lucas's sake, everyone stood up all at once, turned around, and kneeled at their benches for prayer. It was so abrupt; I had to scramble to follow suit. When we got back up, a different minister began what I assumed was another sermon. Then the crowd sang another beautiful, but mournful-sounding hymn.

I had only a few experiences with religion to prepare myself for this. The church I'd been in the most was St. Patrick's Cathedral in New York City, where I stopped in every once in a while, just because it was so beautiful inside. It gave me a feeling of peace. There was a big difference between St. Patrick's and this Amish barn.

As Erma had warned me, I did not understand a word, nor did I enjoy the experience much except for the sheer novelty of it and getting a glimpse now and then of Lucas sitting among the other men. He did not smile at me or acknowledge me in any way, but there was a softening in his face when our eyes met, and I hoped it was a sign that he was pleased I had come.

After about an hour, my back got tired. An hour and a half, and I desperately wished I had something to lean against. At two hours, I understood where the stoicism of the Amish came from. After two and a half hours, my stomach reminded me that I had been in such a hurry this morning that I had foolishly skipped breakfast. This was something I deeply regretted as the preacher droned on in their Germanic language and my watch crept toward hour number three.

This is what my mother experienced throughout her early life. It was difficult to imagine her sitting still this long. Desiree avoided boredom like a cat avoided water.

Toward the end of the service, one man got up and mentioned Prudence's name. I felt Erma tense up beside me. Prudence sat a couple of rows in front of us. At the mention of her name, she bowed her head and seemed to make herself smaller. A stern-looking man I assumed was the bishop said a few words to her, and she nodded miserably a couple times. More words were said, and then I felt Erma relax a little beside me. Apparently, the moment she had been dreading was over.

Although services went on around us, I kept looking at the slumped shoulders of Erma's granddaughter, hoping her family and the church would be kind to her.

Then they began what I thought was probably the ceremony to choose a new minister that Erma had mentioned. This was apparently a very big deal. I could feel the tension in the crowd as five men solemnly walked forward. They each chose one of the five hymnals that had been laid out on a separate bench beforehand.

"What's going on?" I whispered to Erma.

One of the older women who was seated in front of me, hearing my whisper, put a warning finger to her lips. I lapsed into silence.

With my aching back, I waited in ignorance, along with the rest of the church. Even the children stilled, picking up on their parents' tenseness as the five men opened their hymnbooks.

I heard a muffled groan come from one of the five men.

"What is it?" I whispered, risking yet another chastening look from the older woman, but Erma merely frowned and gave a quick shake of her head, warning me to be quiet.

The man who had groaned, staggered outside through a side door with his hand over his mouth. We could hear him outside, retching violently. The four other men looked both relieved and sympathetic, and the congregation continued to sit quietly, waiting.

In a few moments, the man returned. He looked pale and shaky, but he said a few words I found out later were an acceptance of the position and a request that the people pray for him to overcome his many weaknesses so that he could serve them well. He stuttered slightly, but he got the words out.

In a few more minutes, we were dismissed, and it was a solemn group of people who walked out of the barn toward the house, where Erma told me we would all share a meal together in the basement. She had left her pies in my car, so we walked across the field together to get them.

"Do you mind explaining what just happened in there?" I asked.

"Judah Yoder chose the hymnal that had the slip of paper in it, and it upset him."

"What slip of paper?"

"The one that says, 'You have been chosen.'"

"Chosen for what?"

"To be our new minister."

"And that's why he started throwing up?"

"Probably. Judah has always had a nervous stomach when he gets upset."

"He certainly didn't seem very happy about it," I said.

"Of course not. It is a heavy responsibility, and unlike *Englisch* ministers, he will not be paid. This will be a job he will perform on top of running a family business, helping care for his widowed mother, and he just found out this week that his wife is pregnant with their second set of twins."

"No wonder he was upset!"

"I agree. Few men desire it," Erma said. "But they almost always accept it as the Lord's will. Amish men don't walk away from their responsibilities."

I was getting a little tired of hearing about what Amish men would or wouldn't do.

"I don't know," I said. "Some Amish men apparently ride away from their responsibilities and leave their bicycles hidden in the weeds."

"Are you making a joke?" Erma asked.

"Maybe a little one."

"Samuel's disappearance is not funny, Amy."

"Of course it isn't, but didn't you tell me that Samuel had been chosen to participate in this ceremony?"

"Yes," Erma said. "Originally, there were six men being considered. We all thought Samuel would make a fine minister...until he disappeared."

With the sound of Judah retching outside the barn still echoing in my ears, I thought I might have solved the mystery of why Samuel had run away.

"Now that the ceremony is over," I said. "Maybe Samuel will think it's safe to come back."

"That's not funny, either," Erma said. "Please do not make the mistake of treating our customs and our people as entertainment. You really don't know us. Samuel would never shirk his duty like that."

"I wasn't trying to be funny," I said. "But I am confused. I thought your people believed only Jesus was perfect. I didn't realize you thought Samuel was, as well."

I didn't wait for Erma's reply. I opened my SUV's trunk so she could get her Tupperware double pie carrier out of the backseat. I was suddenly sick to death, of all things Amish.

"You are right, and I apologize for my harsh words to you." Erma surprised me by saying. "I do not want to believe what you say about Samuel, and so I lashed out. I'll try not to do that again."

"It's okay, Erma," I said. "We are all worried about him."

"You will eat well today with us." Erma's tone lightened as she changed the subject. "There is always plenty."

I had looked forward to enjoying the meal they had prepared, but now—not so much. "I think I'll go back. Can you find another way home?"

"I can get a ride," Erma said. "But why aren't you going to eat with us? Are you not feeling well?"

"I'm just a little tired," I said. "And I need to get back to work. This week has put me behind on my writing schedule."

"I suppose it's just as well," she said pensively. "Everyone will want to discuss what happened at church and they would feel awkward with an *Englisch* person in our midst."

"Of course, they would." It hurt a little, being reminded that I was still considered a complete outsider to these friends and neighbors. "I understand. Will Prudence be eating with you today?"

"I don't know, but since she has made her confession before the church and asked for forgiveness, she will be welcome." Erma said this stoically, and without warmth.

I thought about the girl's rounded shoulders. "But people will talk about her, anyway?"

"My people are human," Erma said. "They gossip and are not always kind about it."

"Do they gossip about me?"

"Of course," Erma said. "But not as much as if you were part of our church. Don't worry. We don't expect your behavior to be the same as ours."

Instead of reassuring me, her blunt words stung. She was right. I was not one of them. That was the thing about the Amish. We could be friends—even good friends—but an *Englisch* person would never experience the intimacy of being truly a trusted part of their lives.

I carefully drove out of the graveled, circular driveway, dodging Amish children running back and forth, and I headed home feeling foolish for having gone. Lucas's family and church might be helpful and friendly, but I was not part of them. I was fairly certain I never would be, no matter how hard I tried. I could learn to speak fluent Pennsylvania Dutch, wear their style of clothing, take whatever instruction I needed to join their church, and still be considered an outsider for the rest of my life. Their roots with one another went too deep.

After what I had just witnessed with Prudence and the newly appointed minister throwing up outside the barn, I wasn't at all sure I would ever want to be anything more than an outsider!

CHAPTER 37

I went home, tossed my all black ensemble into a pile on the floor, and donned my favorite blue cotton sweater and jeans, which made me feel much better. Then I made a plate of assorted cheese and crackers, boiled water and made tea, put copious amounts of honey in it, and carried it into my quiet office. That was my go-to snack when I needed comfort.

After the emotion and nervousness of the morning, it came as a relief when I sat down at my computer. I would spend the day pushing the story of my heroic World War II nurse forward. Finally, I was back to doing something I was good at and understood.

In a few minutes, I was living in another time and place. Instead of thinking about Lucas and his church, I let myself sink into the deep point of view of a heroic half-starved POW nurse battling a recurrence of malaria while still caring for the sick and wounded. Often, the lives of other people put my petty problems into perspective. This was one of those times.

That afternoon, I got nearly three thousand words written before someone knocked on the back door. Since I was in my writing fog, I was slow to respond. Most people who knocked on the back door did so only as a polite warning before they stuck their head in and hollered "hello" anyway.

I finally realized there really was someone waiting for me to open the back door, so I did. I was not prepared for what was on the other side.

"Excuse me, but do you know where Lucas is?" the man asked. "He isn't in the *Daadi Haus* or barn."

I had walked to the door in a partial writing fog, busy forming my next sentence. The next minute, I threw my hand over my mouth to keep from gasping. Staring at me from the other side of the screen stood Gretchen's missing husband.

"Samuel!" I said, astonished. "Where on earth have you been? Does Gretchen know you're here?"

"Excuse me." He took a step back. "I know you are Rick's step-daughter, but I have forgotten your name."

"I'm Amy Stanton." I opened the screen door and stepped out onto the porch. "We met briefly when you purchased a pony from Lucas."

He took another step back. I was half afraid he'd bolt, and we'd never see him again, so I tried to act like he was just another visitor—not the man we'd all been so worked up about.

"I'm sure Lucas will be here shortly. Please come in and have a seat. Are you thirsty? Hungry?"

The whole time I was speaking, I had an entirely different conversation going on in my head.

Why did you abandon your wife and kids without so much as a word? Don't you realize Gretchen is pregnant and those sweet little girls cry at night for you to come home? What kind of man does that, huh? Huh?

Instead, I said, "I have lemonade. Would you like some?"

He seemed uncertain.

"You can wait on the porch for Lucas." My voice was honeyed. "He should arrive home soon."

"Do you know where he is?"

He's probably trying to help his sister with chores around your farm, you jerk!

"I think he might have gone to visit a relative after church," I said. "Would you prefer some iced tea?"

"No, thank you. Did he go to visit my wife and children by any chance?" he asked nervously.

It was at that moment Lucas rode in on his horse wearing his Sunday best. I was glad to see him because I didn't know what to do with Samuel, but honestly, no man should look as good as Lucas did on horseback. Having realized just that morning that I could never become Amish, not even for him, the sight broke my heart.

Lucas didn't greet his brother-in-law immediately. Instead, he got off his horse, tied it to a post, and joined us on the porch. To me, his actions seemed unnecessarily unhurried. I realized he was holding back on his anger. Giving himself time to adjust to Samuel's presence. The memory of his bloodied knuckles when he'd driven his hands into the wall of the barn came to mind. It was probably wise for him to take the time to get his anger at his brother-in-law in check before greeting him.

The Amish do shake hands, but Lucas didn't. Nor did he hug his brother-in-law or even smile. Instead, he went directly to the core of the matter. "Where have you been?"

I stood in the doorway awaiting Samuel's answer, but Lucas glanced at me and gave an almost imperceptible movement of his head, which I knew meant he wanted me to leave.

So, I left. But I didn't go very far. Nor did I close the door. Considering the miles I'd put on my car trying to find Samuel, I felt justified in leaning against the kitchen counter, out of sight, but well within earshot. Fortunately, I have excellent hearing.

Good hearing, however, doesn't make up for the inability to understand their language. Those two Amish men immediately lapsed into Pennsylvania Dutch, and I couldn't understand a thing. This was annoying. I vowed to become fluent.

Finally, the talking stopped, and they left together. Lucas said nothing to me about where Samuel had been or where they were going. Why should he?

After all, I was just an *Englisch* outsider.

CHAPTER 38

I t rained soon after Lucas and Samuel left. It was a warm, slow, spring rain that made my office feel cozy when I went back to work. I had lost the flow of my story, but I still had a thousand words left to write if I were to meet my weekly goal.

I'd just finished the words and was in the process of closing my computer when the phone rang. I saw the word DAD appear on my phone.

"Hi there," I said. My grin was so wide I knew he could hear it in my voice.

"Whatcha doing?" Brady said, with an exaggerated drawl.

"I just now finished up work," I said. "What about you?"

"Oh, nothing much. I was popping some popcorn and thinking about watching an old John Wayne movie."

"That sounds nice." I settled into my office's comfy chair.

"It would be a lot nicer if I had my favorite daughter here to watch it with me."

"I'd really like that." I'd never meant anything more.

"Look out your back window," he said.

"Why?"

"Just go look."

I ran to the kitchen window and there, parked behind my house, was my dad waving from the door of his RV.

"Brady!" I yelled into the phone, as excited as a kid at Christmas. "When did you get here?"

"I pulled in about ten minutes ago. I'm surprised you didn't hear me."

"The rain on the roof must have covered up the sound."

"Doesn't matter. Come on over, neighbor!"

"No! You come over here!"

"Another time. I've already got the movie ready, and the popcorn popped."

I didn't even bother with a raincoat or umbrella. I slid my feet into a pair of rain boots and ran straight to his RV. He was waiting with a bear hug and the place indeed smelled of popcorn.

It wasn't until he released me from his hug that I saw the black eye. It was quite a shiner.

I gently touched his cheek. "What happened? Did you get into a fight?"

"Not with anything human." He laughed it off. "Big ole bull zigged when I expected him to zag. Doctor said another half inch and I would have lost an eye. But it wasn't, and I didn't. So, enough about that. I drove a hundred miles out of my way just to see a movie with my daughter. I need to leave early tomorrow morning, so let's get started!"

The black eye dampened my excitement a bit, but he seemed to be in a festive mood and I didn't want to spoil it for him. After all, I had a father, and he'd just driven out of his way to spend time with me.

He held out a tub of fresh popcorn. "Do you want parmesan cheese on yours? Or pepper? Or both?"

"How did you know I like my popcorn with parmesan and pepper on it?" I asked.

"It was a wild guess. Darla always liked hers that way, and kids usually end up liking what their moms like because that's what she feeds them. Have you been in touch with her? Does she know we met?"

Darla Sanders. There was so much my dad didn't know. It was tempting to unburden myself about my shocking new knowledge about Desiree, but I knew anything said couldn't be unsaid. I had concluded that it wouldn't be fair to talk to anyone about her until I'd talked to her.

"I haven't called her yet," I said. "I'm still working things out in my head about what to say."

"Good luck." He cracked open a soda for himself and another one for me. "We're gonna watch The Big Trail. It's one of my favorites. I've seen it more times than I can count. Does that sound good to you?"

"Sure!"

Once the movie started, he muted it, took a swig out of his soda can, and said, "So, how's everything going for you?"

"I thought you wanted to watch the movie."

"Sure. I want to watch it, but that doesn't mean I want to listen to it. I already know every word they're saying. Why don't you tell me about that Amish man you were with when we met?"

And so, I told my father everything about me and Lucas. Even about the trip to the Amish church earlier in the day. I talked for nearly an hour and not once did he seem to lose interest. It was like he was just soaking it up. I finally ran out of words, and I wasn't sure what to expect. I hadn't really given him a lot of room to say anything.

"Sorry," I said. "I didn't mean to go on and on like that."

"I loved every second," he said. "Am I allowed to act like a real dad now?"

"Of course you may act like a real dad," I said. "You are a real dad!"

"Well, sweetie," he said. "You've made me sad."

"How?"

"It's the thought of a smart, pretty girl like you, thinking she has to turn Amish just to convince a man to marry her. There's not one blasted thing about you that needs changing, sweetheart. You're already perfect."

Those words felt indescribably sweet. I closed my eyes and savored them. My father thought I was perfect.

"But if I don't change, he'll go find some Amish woman and marry her."

"So what? You'll find someone better. What you deserve is a man who'll love you so much he'll beg you to marry him no matter what."

"But…"

"Don't argue with your old dad, Amy. I've met plenty of women down through the years and let me tell you something—you are a prize and don't you ever forget it." He toasted me with his soda can.

"I had never been inside an RV until I met you." I took my empty popcorn bowl and sat it in the sink. "It's about the size of my apartment in New York, except the space is better arranged."

"And I've never been inside a New York City apartment," Brady said. "I know what it's like to live within a prison cell, though."

"Is this a good time to tell me about why you were in prison?" I hoped he wouldn't be upset about me asking, but I needed to know.

He ran his hand back through his hair, and his expression hardened. "I suppose you have the right to know."

"Whatever it is, it won't make a difference to me," I hastily reassured him. "I promise."

"Well… I never killed anybody, if that's what you're wondering, but I came close"

"Okay." I nodded to encourage him to continue.

"After I finally got out of that wheelchair, I was still in constant pain. I helped around the ranch and drank to help manage the pain, which was stupid, but I didn't know what else to do. Around 2003, I'd piled up too many DUIs, and the judge was sick of it. He sent me to prison for a while to keep me from accidentally killing myself or somebody else.

"Prison is supposed to be bad, but it was especially hard for a cowboy like me who was used to being outside. After I sobered up, I thought I'd lose my mind. It made me sit and stare at a prison wall, and that forced me to admit to myself what I'd become.

"That's when things changed. I'd never been religious, but my folks always took me to church when I was a kid. It's amazing how important the gospel looks when you're stuck in the bottom of a well and the only light you can see is up. That's what it felt like. So, I changed. It was a slow process, but I came out of prison a better man than went in. A big part of that involved letting go of the anger I had toward your mother. I decided it was too heavy to carry around anymore."

We sat quietly while his words settled down around me and I examined them one by one. I'd been carrying a lot of anger and resentment toward Desiree, too, and Brady was right—it was heavy.

"As my release date got closer," Brady continued, "I tried to figure out what to do with the rest of my life. My folks had lost the ranch by then. I figured the one marketable skill I had left was a knack for reading animal behavior. I knew I couldn't ride the bulls any longer, but I thought I had a chance of making a living bullfighting at rodeos. The money is pretty good if you're top tier, but it takes a while. The trick is staying alive long enough to get good at it."

"But it couldn't have been easy getting started," I said. "I've seen documentaries on how hard it is to get work straight out of prison."

Brady chuckled. "People don't expect bullfighters to be choir boys, and I had connections from my riding days. The Bull Riding Championship helped.

"2005 to 2010 were the rebuilding years. Just local stuff, working my way up. By 2011, I was back on the professional circuit. Got my first major sponsorship in 2013, and I've been on the top tier since about 2015."

"So, you've been at the peak of your career for about ten years?"

"Thereabouts.

"How often do you work?" I hoped it wasn't too often. The job was dangerous.

"I do up to ten rodeos a week during peak season, and I travel sixty to seventy thousand miles a year. I refuse to do any more than that because fatigue can get you killed."

"How do you keep from being scared all the time?" I leaned forward, really wanting to know the answer.

"I do everything I can to lessen the danger. I work with a sports trainer, and I keep a couple of national gym memberships current so I can work out every chance I get, no matter what town I find myself in. I take kick boxing lessons during the off season. Staying strong and light-footed makes a big difference. The rest of my time, I watch videos of myself figuring out ways to improve, and I study other rodeo bullfighters."

"Do your clown clothes ever get in the way?"

"Nope. Those wild-colored clothes have a purpose. They distract the bull's attention. Under that clothing, we wear protective body gear. So do the bull riders, only they keep their gear to a minimum and only wear what will fit beneath their cowboy pants and shirts. Because of our clothing, we can wear a lot more padding and Kevlar."

"So that's why you could walk out of there the other night instead of being carried," I said.

"It helped. The clown's makeup is just there to entertain little kids and maybe make the rodeo not such a scary thing for them. Faith is important, too, at least for me," He said this without the slightest sign of embarrassment. "I pray a lot before I go out into the arena. I think most of us do."

"How long do you expect to keep working?"

"Few bullfighters my age are still working the big shows. Most of 'em transition to coaching or training younger guys." He gazed thoughtfully at the John Wayne movie, that was still playing silently. "Might be time for me to think about doing that, too. Can't dance with bulls forever."

We talked about both of our lives until the old movie was over. There was a lot of ground to cover. My dad turned the TV off when

196

the movie finished. He needed to get some sleep so he could get an early start. I offered to make him breakfast, but he declined.

"You sleep in," he said. "I'll honk the horn as I drive by. I'll stay longer next time, but I had to come tonight just to convince myself that you were real."

"Please be careful," I said again. "Now that I've found you, I don't think I could bear it if I lost you."

"Nah, I'm tough as an old hickory tree. Nothing's gonna happen to me."

"Well, just make sure it doesn't."

As I ran back through the rain to my house, I saw that Lucas's light was on in the *Daadi Haus*. Apparently, he'd not felt inclined to interrupt my time with my father, and I was glad he hadn't.

CHAPTER 39

Brady tapped his horn as he drove out of my driveway at three-thirty in the morning. I worried about the fact that he had gotten so little sleep before making another long drive, but I was grateful for his quick visit. It was exactly what I'd needed. I hoped it was what he'd needed, too.

Once I heard him leave, I couldn't go back to sleep even if it was the middle of the night, so I got up, threw a robe over my pajamas, fixed some coffee and had just settled down on the back porch swing to think things through, when Lucas showed up.

"Did you make extra?" he said.

"Help yourself." I gestured toward the kitchen.

He disappeared inside, returning moments later to settle beside me on the swing. The wooden slats creaked under his weight, and the familiar scent of the soap he used, mingled with the damp earth smell after the rain.

"That was your dad's RV here last night."

"Yes, it was," I said.

"Did you have a good visit?"

"We did."

In the past, I'd always been the chatter box when it came to making conversation with Lucas. He tended to be more of the strong, silent type. This morning, I figured he'd have to keep the conversation going, if he wanted one.

Apparently, he felt no need to break the silence. Neither did I. The rain had stopped, and the stars were out. The early spring morning felt fresh with possibilities. We sipped our coffee and gazed at the stars.

"Stars are so unchanging," he said. "It gives me a feeling of peace to look at them."

I refrained from telling him that the starlight he was admiring could have been emitted by a star millions of years earlier that no longer existed. Having that sort of knowledge and sharing it might be considered prideful by the Amish, so I kept quiet and let him enjoy his unchanging starlight.

"You left the church yesterday without staying to eat with us," he said. "Why?"

"I had work to do."

"Erma said you seemed a little upset."

A bat swooped low across the yard, hunting for insects in the pre-dawn darkness. I watched its erratic flight, buying time before answering.

"What could possibly make me upset?" I felt my resolve to be quiet dissolving. "Watching a teenage girl being humiliated and listening to a grown man throw his guts up because he's being forced to take on a job he doesn't want was a real hoot. I can hardly wait to go back for another dose."

It was the first time since we'd met that I'd truly pushed back at him about anything. The swing stopped moving as he digested this for a few minutes. I could literally hear crickets chirping. There tend to be lots of them here in the spring.

"I know things like that can seem a little harsh for outsiders who are not used to our culture," he said. "But our ways have worked well for hundreds of years."

He was using the same tone I'd often heard him use to calm a nervous horse. It irritated me he was using it with me now. I shifted to the far end of the swing, putting distance between us.

"If you say so."

"We cannot act as though what Prudence has done is nothing. There are other teenage girls in our church watching. There are plenty of non-Amish boys who consider Amish girls a challenge and walk away when they are finished with them. Judah will grow into his role as minister, while the church shows patience and helps him care for his family responsibilities. You are only looking at our church service through English eyes."

"That's the only eyes I have, Lucas."

A chill breeze swept across the porch, and I pulled my robe tighter around me. It was the closest we had ever had to an argument, and my head pounded from the tension. I didn't know for sure what Lucas wanted from me. Whatever it was, I was pretty certain it was more than I could or should give.

"I'm not ready to talk about this right now, Lucas," I said. "I'm still processing everything."

He nodded, his face half in shadow. The swing moved again as he pushed gently with one foot.

"Would you prefer to know about Samuel?" he asked. "I went with him to see Gretchen."

I tucked my cold feet beneath me, grateful for the change of subject. "Are they still speaking to one another?"

"They are," he said. "They were speaking to one another so loudly; I took the little girls to my mother and father's for the rest of the afternoon so the children wouldn't have to hear their parents' discussion. Gretchen is usually a contented woman. It takes a lot to make her angry, but she has a temper if she is pushed hard enough. Samuel pushed her too hard. It was not a peaceful day for anyone."

The first hint of dawn touched the eastern sky, a barely perceptible lightning of the darkness. Lucas's profile became clearer as I watched him.

"So, what's his story? Does he realize the damage he caused?"

"I don't think he cares. He is in another place in his mind right now. He believes God has spoken to him and given him a calling. He wants to follow it, and I don't think anything Gretchen says—no matter how loudly—will make him turn from it."

"So, what is this calling?"

Lucas leaned forward, elbows on his knees. "The woman who visited him at the sawmill was Dr. Helen Markova. She was the head physician at Shriners Hospital in Erie while Samuel lived nearby with his English uncle and worked there as an orderly. He had not yet made the choice to become Amish. The doctor remembered him as having a special gift with the children."

A rooster crowed in the distance, startling me. "Why did she come to the sawmill? Why not his house?"

"She didn't have his address. But soon after he married Gretchen, he wrote to Dr. Markova to give her notice, letting her know he would not be coming back. He told her about his marriage, and his new job at the sawmill. The doctor had not kept the letter, but remembered thinking it was a waste for a man with his rare skill with sick children to work at a sawmill. She recently had her secretary call the sawmills in the area until she found him."

"So, he left just because a doctor remembered him?"

Lucas shook his head, his eyes reflecting the dim light. "No, she came to tell him that a child he used to care for had passed away. A young girl named Miriam had severe spinal injuries. Samuel spent many hours with the child during her treatments and surgeries. Apparently, before she died, she asked to see him, but they couldn't locate him in time."

"That's heartbreaking," I said, my throat tightening.

"Dr. Markova told Samuel that the hospital was expanding their physical therapy department and wondered if he would ever consider returning to work with children."

I straightened, suddenly understanding. "So, he just... left? To go to work at a hospital? Without first talking it over with Gretchen?"

"He knew she wouldn't want him to go. That's why he borrowed money from his brother instead of taking it out of their savings account."

"Samuel sounds like a bit of a coward," I said.

"Most people are," Lucas said, turning to look at me directly. "It is the easy way. It's choosing to be brave that is hard."

I couldn't argue with that.

"He wrote her a note," Lucas continued, running his hand along the weathered arm of the swing. "Left it on the table where she would find it, but she didn't."

"Are you sure he left one, or is he just saying that to keep her from being as angry with him?"

"No, he wrote it. Usually Gretchen gets up early, but Laura had a stomachache the night before, and Gretchen hadn't gotten a lot of sleep. That's why she stayed in bed that morning a little longer. While she slept, little Laura, the three-year-old, awoke and decided she wanted to draw. For that, she needed paper. She saw her *Daett's* note, turned it over and used the back to draw pictures on. Samuel looked for it to prove he'd written one and found the note beneath her bed with crayon scribbles all over it."'s

"Oh, dear." I sighed. "That sweet child. Is she okay?"

"They weren't harsh with her. Gretchen blamed herself for sleeping in."

Lucas stood and walked to the edge of the porch, staring out at the farm as the shadows slowly retreated before the coming day. His broad shoulders carried the weight of his family's troubles.

"When he arrived in Erie, Dr. Markova showed him around the new children's wing. There was a little boy there who was severely ill, refusing treatment, not responding to anyone. The staff was at their wits' end, and so were his parents. Samuel somehow got through to him when no one else could. After that, one day became two, then a week as the boy healed."

A mockingbird began its morning repertoire, the complex song cutting through the stillness. I rose from the swing and joined Lucas at the railing, keeping a careful distance between us.

"What did Samuel live on all this time? The money his brother gave him wouldn't be enough to cover his expenses and to send those money orders. How did he support himself?"

"The hospital offered him a temporary position—just basic care work, nothing that required certification. He took it, planning to earn enough to return home soon. But the more time he spent there, the more convinced he became that this was his calling."

I tapped my fingers against the wooden railing. "And he didn't bother letting Gretchen know?"

"I think you mentioned that my brother-in-law is a coward? Telling Gretchen over the phone what he was doing wasn't something he could face yet. At least not until he'd decided what he was going to do. When that little boy's health turned around, he made his decision and came home."

"And now?"

Lucas turned toward me, the first rays of sunlight illuminating his face. "Now he's having to explain to Gretchen why he believes God is calling him to move to Erie so he can serve these sick children. He wants her and the girls to go with him, of course, but Gretchen does not want to go."

I nodded, understanding at last the gravity of the situation and why Lucas had seemed so troubled lately. The sun continued its slow ascent, gradually bringing light to the world. A new day was beginning, but for Samuel and Gretchen, their future had never been more uncertain.

CHAPTER 40

This was big news. Amish people moved to new places all the time, but Lucas's family seemed entrenched in the Sugarcreek area. It would be heartbreaking for everyone if Gretchen and the children moved so far away.

"What makes Samuel so good with sick children that a doctor would drive all the way to Sugarcreek to recruit him?" I asked.

Lucas leaned back against the porch railing. "At the Shriner's Hospital, his job was simple—he transported children from one place in the hospital to another. He was young and strong and could lift them easily, even the older ones. He also loves to whistle and can mimic a lot of different birds perfectly. The children loved that, and they loved him."

As he spoke, Lucas's usually reserved expression softened, as if picturing his brother-in-law in this role.

"He says they would hear him coming down the hallways and would call out to him. They nicknamed him the 'birdie man.' When he wasn't needed to transport them, he would spend hours with the sicker ones, reading to them, talking to them, playing little games with them—especially those whose families couldn't be there all the time.

The hospital staff noted that the children Samuel spent time with were calmer, withstood pain better, and invariably recuperated faster."

"Why did he ever leave?"

"Gretchen." Lucas pushed away from the railing. "He came back home for a relative's wedding, saw my sister who was all grown up, and he fell head-over-heels for the little girl he'd ignored in grade school."

A hint of brotherly protectiveness crossed Lucas's face.

"He came back to Ohio to court her and got that job at the sawmill. His heart has never been in lumber, though. He told me he couldn't stop thinking about the children at the hospital and how much he could accomplish there versus spending his life turning logs into lumber. He longed to go back, but it took the doctor coming to see him that caused him to realize how much."

"So now he wants to go back to the same job he had when he was young?" The wood of the porch floor was cool beneath my bare feet. I wished I had put on my thick socks.

"He wants to do a lot more than that." Lucas's eyes lit up with what almost looked like admiration. "Dr. Markova offered to find the funds to help Samuel become a physical therapist's assistant. It will take about two years for him to become certified. In the meantime, the hospital is offering him a job doing what he did before until he can get his certification."

"It sounds like a wonderful opportunity," I said. "And it's what, less than three hours away? I don't see why Gretchen and the children can't move there with him and come back for plenty of visits with her family and friends."

Lucas's hand closed around one of the porch posts, his knuckles whitening. "Except for one big problem," he said. "Samuel thinks they might need to leave the Amish."

"Wait. What?" I straightened, suddenly alert. "Why would he have to do that? Taking care of sick and physically disabled children doesn't sound like something the Amish would forbid one of their members to do."

"True, nor is it forbidden to achieve various certifications to get work. But it is nearly impossible for an Amish person to work full time and raise a family within a city environment while still adhering to the Amish principles of driving horses and buggies and going without electricity." Lucas traced a weathered groove in the post with his thumb. "There are Amish communities outside the area, but it isn't feasible to fellowship with them regularly or to keep a horse and buggy for transportation."

"Oh." I hadn't thought of it that way.

"Exactly," Lucas said. "It is very hard to remain Amish outside of an Amish settlement."

I wrapped my arms around myself, suddenly chilled. "What's going to happen, Lucas?"

He shook his head, his eyes troubled. "Nobody knows. Gretchen is putting up more resistance than he expected. My sister fears for the souls of their children. She has been taught most of her life that the church is the ark of salvation. The concept of anyone being saved outside of our church is impossible for her to accept. Samuel believes God gave him a gift for healing, has opened doors and created an opportunity, and that it would be a sin not to use it."

"In other words, it's a mess." I bit my lower lip, thinking of those little girls caught between their parents' conflicting beliefs.

"Yes. Samuel has put our church and our family in a terrible position." Lucas's shoulders slumped slightly, bearing an invisible weight.

I felt a surge of indignation. "I disagree," I said, taking a step toward him. "It is not Samuel who has put everyone in a terrible position—he is simply trying to obey God the best he knows how. In my eyes, it is the rules your church has layered onto this young couple that are causing the trouble. Taking care of crippled children is not the act of a selfish man. Samuel and his family should not be punished for it."

Lucas's expression hardened. "Again," he said evenly, "you are looking at this only through English eyes. You cannot possibly understand the ramifications."

I felt my own temper flare. "And once again, let me remind you that English eyes are the only kind I have."

We were at an impasse. The sun was fully risen now, casting long shadows across the porch as Lucas and I stood facing each other, the tension between us real.

"I wonder if Samuel knew," I said.

"Knew what?" Lucas asked, his voice guarded.

"That he might be selected as minister. Erma mentioned he was one of the candidates before he disappeared."

Lucas was quiet for so long, I thought he might not answer. He walked to the far end of the porch and stared out at the fields, his back to me.

"Samuel would have made an excellent minister," he finally said, still not turning around. "He has—had—a gift for reaching people, for understanding their struggles."

A trio of crows flew overhead, their harsh calls a stark contrast to the beauty of the morning.

"Do you think that influenced his decision to leave? The possibility of being chosen?" I asked.

Lucas turned to face me then. "If you are asking whether Samuel ran away from his duty, the answer is no. If anything, I believe he simply felt called to a different ministry."

"But the timing..."

"The timing suggests a man wrestling with his purpose, yes." Lucas crossed the distance between us, his steps deliberate. "Our church calls men to serve as ministers without regard to their wishes. In the weeks before a new minister is chosen, the candidates are encouraged to search their hearts, to ensure they are worthy of the calling should it come to them."

"And Samuel was searching his heart?"

"Yes. Perhaps too deeply." Lucas said. "I think when Dr. Markova appeared with news of that child's death, it struck Samuel as a sign—a divine message about where his true calling lay."

"Do you think he's right? That God wants him serving at that hospital instead of staying here?" I watched Lucas's face carefully.

"It is not for me to say where another man's calling lies. I only know that when Samuel spoke of those children at the hospital, his face shone with the same light I've seen in our most devoted ministers when they speak of God."

"Yet your church will shun him if he leaves." I couldn't keep the edge from my voice.

"Yes. That is our way." Lucas's voice was heavy with resignation. "We cannot keep our community strong if we allow members to simply leave when they find aspects of our life too difficult, or think they'd like to try a different kind of life."

I stepped closer, unable to let this go. "But couldn't his work at the hospital be seen as ministry, too? Isn't caring for the suffering what Jesus did?"

A flash of something—doubt perhaps—crossed Lucas's features before his expression settled into its familiar stoicism. "These are the very questions Samuel is asking. And Gretchen must decide if she can follow him into that ministry, or if her own calling is to remain within our community."

"No simple answers," I said.

"No," Lucas agreed. "Only difficult choices."

He took a deep breath, as if gathering courage. "I was wrong to ask you to consider becoming Amish," he said. "Please forgive me. I had forgotten how different we are, and how difficult it would be for you to understand our ways."

The words hit me like a physical blow. I took an involuntary step back, my hand finding the porch railing for support.

"There is nothing to forgive," I said, wondering how many times and how many ways this man could break my heart. The gulf between us was too great. I could not change my life that much without resentment. Not even for Lucas. And Lucas? He had never intended to change at all.

It was going to be one of the hardest things I had ever done, but my dad's words kept playing in my mind over and over: "You deserve a man who will love you so much that he will beg you to marry him exactly like you are. You are a prize and don't you forget it."

I lifted my chin, steeling myself for what I knew I needed to do. "I think it would be best for me to go back to Manhattan for a while."

Lucas's expression shifted to alarm. "Because of this?" he said. "Please don't. You belong here, you love it here."

"I love it here," I agreed, the beauty around us making the admission even more painful. "But Erma made a point of reminding me yesterday that your people are none of my business. I now realize how very right she is. I need to get away from you and other Amish for a while."

I left him then. I went inside and closed the door with a soft click that somehow felt louder than a slam in its finality. Lucas deserved a good Amish wife who would understand and comply with all the rules and regulations. I was not that woman, nor could I ever be. The price I would have to pay was too high for both of us.

CHAPTER 41

Sugarcreek is beautiful in the spring, but Central Park in New York City is also beautiful. Suddenly, I was hungry to spend time with my own people where I understood the rules. Fortunately, I had not let go of my apartment, so it was still there waiting to welcome me. I did not intend to come back for quite a while. I knew Lucas would take good care of everything while I was gone.

Two suitcases later, I trundled them down the stairs, thinking that the sooner I could leave, the better. I was emotionally drained, and I had a long drive ahead of me. The sun was just starting to peek over the beautiful horizon.

I was fine until I got to the porch where Lucas and I had spent so many hours making plans for the farm. He was standing beside the porch table upon which was an enormous bouquet of yellow and white daffodils in a chipped, white pail of water. They were gorgeous.

"These are the first daffodils of the season," Lucas said. "There's a place down by the creek where they always bloom early. There used to be an old house down there, but only the foundation remains now. I had wanted you to see them, but since you are leaving, I brought them to you."

Lucas had once again taken my breath away. I wished he would stop doing that. The only way I could survive him bringing another woman home with him was to stop loving him, and here he was, making it difficult again.

"They are beautiful." I buried my face in the bouquet. They were still covered in dew. The sweet scent was lovely. "I didn't know daffodils could smell like that."

"These are the old-fashioned ones," he said. "Smaller than the commercial kind. They haven't had the scent bred out of them."

He had his hands in his pockets, watching me.

"Thank you, Lucas," I said. "You are a thoughtful man."

"Apparently not always," he said. "But I'll take your suitcases out to the car if you are still determined to go."

"I have to." I tried to keep my voice light. "No offense, my friend, but I really don't want to be here when you bring home that wonderful Amish wife you are going to be searching for."

He closed his eyes as though my words hurt, but he didn't correct or reassure me. He just grabbed both of my suitcases by their handles and carried them out to the trunk of my car. Being Lucas, he didn't bother with dragging them along on their wheels. He was so strong he just picked them up and carried them.

"May God be with you and keep you safe," he said, as I climbed into my driver's seat. "I checked the oil and tires. You only have a quarter tank of gas, so it would be wise to get some more before you leave town."

He wasn't making it any easier to leave, being so solicitous and kind, but I knew I had to. There really was no choice. I cared too much for him. But I cared about myself, too. I had to leave while I was still upset enough to pull away.

"Thank you, Lucas."

He nodded once, acknowledging my thanks, then he stepped back and allowed me to drive away.

CHAPTER 42

New York City
Four months later
I celebrated my twenty-ninth birthday by turning in my final draft of Iron Angel. It had been easier to concentrate on my work when the only thing I had to look at as I wrote was a brick wall six feet away outside my window. I thought it was a good book. My editor was happy with it. We were going to meet the next day for lunch to celebrate.

I hoped the family of that amazing World War II nurse would be pleased with my treatment of their grandmother's story. I liked the title they chose. The soldiers called the nurses who cared for them the "Angels of Bataan" and with good reason.

For three years, while in captivity and experiencing malaria, dysentery, and starvation themselves, those Army and Navy nurses cared for the sick and wounded in strict four-hour shifts. The nurses who survived the POW prison camp made certain they were always dressed in the best sort of uniform they could pull together, even when those uniforms weren't much more than rags. They had rounds and responsibilities, even when there was no medicine, and no food, and the only thing the nurses had to give was the comfort of their presence.

Toward the end, it often took a will of iron for them to even rise from their beds and walk upright, let alone continue to care for others.

After it was all over and they had been rescued by the allies, they and the doctors who treated them realized that their routine and sense of purpose had kept them going when others had given up. A strict routine and purpose had saved their lives.

I would have liked to think I could be as strong as they were if I were put in that position, but I doubted it. However, writing about my heroine's determination to adhere to a routine had helped me survive my own crisis. Sticking to a strict writing routine was the only thing that got me out of bed those first rough weeks after leaving Lucas and Sugarcreek.

Discipline, routine, and purpose were powerful things. It could save a life. In a way, it was saving mine.

And so... I no longer allowed myself to get up when I felt like it and lounge around in my pajamas in front of my computer all day. After wallowing in self-pity for a couple of days after I arrived back in New York, I started setting my alarm, getting out of bed, showering, and dressing. I was usually sitting at my desk typing or editing by seven o'clock most mornings. Whether or not I felt like it.

It bothered me that I had not yet been able to return the Sotheby items Rick stole. Those items had been the last thing on my mind when I packed to leave. But they had been missing for years. I thought they could wait a few more months.

I did intend to go back to Sugarcreek, but not any time soon. I truly wanted Lucas to be happy. He was a man who needed a houseful of children to love and protect. I wanted him to find someone with whom he could build a family, and I also knew that couldn't be me. I intended to stay in New York for the time being. It would give him the freedom to do what he needed to do, and it would give me the freedom to heal.

I went out on a date last night. A friend of a friend who was visiting the city. The man was pleasant enough, but the evening was completely forgettable, and that was okay. What was important was that I was going on with my life.

Come late fall, when the rodeo circuit slacked off, Dad and I were planning to go meet my grandparents. I did not have the words to describe how much I was looking forward to that.

I had not seen or talked to Desiree in weeks. It wasn't deliberate. She got the part she wanted in the Ron Howard movie. It was a role for a woman in her late forties that would use all of her acting skills. I was proud of her for embracing her age on the screen. This movie was so important for her career, I didn't want to upset her by bringing up the contents of Rick's letter. I would wait until it was over—and then invite her to come here so we could spend some time together. She loved New York City, so maybe we could talk then.

I wasn't ready for that conversation yet either. My feelings about Desiree had transformed since learning about her past—not simpler, but deeper. The angry child in me wanted to confront her and demand explanations for every lie. But the adult I'd become understood that her story was so much more complex than I once thought.

From Dorcas Schlabach to Darla Sanders to Desiree Stanton—each identity was a step away from pain, a desperate bid for control over her own life. I couldn't forget what she did to Brady, but I also couldn't ignore the courage it took to build herself anew, to keep moving forward despite having no one to rely on but herself.

And despite everything, she kept me. Raised me. In her self-absorbed, erratic way, she loved me. That counted for something.

When we talked, I wanted it to be a conversation, not a confrontation.

I tried not to think about Sugarcreek. It would have been easier if not for the handwritten letters I received from Lucas. I had no choice but to open them. There could be decisions or information about the farm I needed to know. He never called me. He simply wrote these letters, and they had been a revelation. That rustic Amish farmer with an eighth-grade education was a surprisingly good writer.

It was the strangest thing. When we were together, we had friendly conversations—but never about the things he was putting in these letters. These were not love letters to me. Instead, they seemed to be love letters to the universe in which he found himself.

He described the feeling of breaking new ground with his Belgians with such vivid imagery I could practically smell the scent of fresh-turned earth. He talked about the precious, tiny, pale blue eggs of the Eastern Bluebird with such love that it felt like a poem. There were vignettes about his interactions with the various people of Sugarcreek that were so riveting and entertaining, it made me long to go back and live among those gentle, puzzling people again.

I had such mixed feelings about these letters. I thought it would be best if I didn't read them, and yet the moment I got one, I couldn't stop myself from ripping it open and sinking back into his world.

Not a word about his search for a wife, of course. Even though he must have known I was eaten up with curiosity and dread, he mentioned nothing about that.

Sometimes I walked the blocks from my apartment to St. Patrick's Cathedral. I found peace there in the glow of those beautiful stained-glass windows, a peace I hoped came from a loving God. I sometimes wondered if the Lord of miracles might find time one day to make my heart stop aching for a man I had to stop loving if I was ever to know true happiness again.

CHAPTER 43

I was with my editor at the Palm Court at the Plaza Hotel when my phone buzzed. I ignored it. She and I were having a pleasant lunch while talking about possibilities for our next writing project, and I didn't want to be interrupted, so I didn't answer.

I selected a tiny, crustless, cucumber sandwich from the finger foods displayed on the tray beside us and nibbled it while refilling my delicate teacup with the pot of hot tea sitting in front of my plate. I'd chosen the Plaza's Signature Blend, and it was delicious. My editor had the Chai Imperial and the spicy aroma wafting from it had me wishing I had chosen that one instead. Maybe next time.

My cell phone buzzed again.

I'd been getting a lot of scam calls recently, so I ignored it. If it was important, whoever it was would leave a message.

"I'm sorry, Amy. I have to leave you for a few minutes," my editor said, apologetically. "This tea is going straight through me."

"Of course," I said. "Please take your time."

Going to the restroom from the Palm Court was a bit of a trek. There was a long corridor, a stairwell leading down to the basement, and then more walking. I felt sorry for anyone who needed to get there quickly.

I was pouring another cup of tea when the phone buzzed a third time. That worried me enough to dig my cell phone out of my purse and glance at the number. The area code was 330, which meant it could be someone calling from Sugarcreek. My pulse quickened as I answered it.

It was Erma.

"I don't know if I should make this call," she said. "It's probably a mistake, but Lucas…"

She choked up and my heart tightened with fear.

"What about Lucas?"

"He's been hurt."

"What do you mean? What happened?"

"Well." Erma took a deep breath and started in. "Ida Schrock came to town with her daughter, Charity. Ida has dementia, and Charity can't hardly do a thing with her anymore, poor thing. She's afraid to leave her mother at home alone, but taking her with her to do errands is getting iffy."

"Tell me about Lucas, Erma."

"That's what I'm trying to do!" Erma said. "Ida refused to get out of the buggy. She's been getting combative recently. Charity ran in to get some groceries, but Ida was tired of waiting and decided she wanted to go home. She got out of the buggy, untied the horse, got back in, and headed out. She's still spry enough to do things like that, even if her mind doesn't work good anymore."

"But Lucas?"

"Charity and her husband had just gotten this new standard bred horse a week ago, and he hadn't had time to settle yet. Ida made him go into the wrong lane. You know how much fast traffic there always is on Route 93. The oncoming cars were dodging around Ida, but a lot of them were blowing their horns. That confused her even more, and it really frightened the horse. Next thing you know, that animal was galloping down the highway completely out of control and Ida was bouncing around all over that buggy trying to hang on."

"What's Lucas got to do with this?" I practically shouted, trying to get Erma to skip the details. "Is he okay?"

"No! He's not okay! That's what I'm trying to tell you." Erma paused a moment, as though gathering her thoughts, and then continued. "Lucas was riding into town on that black stallion of his, and heard the car horns, and saw all the commotion and tried to do something about it. You know how good he is with horses. He probably figured his big saddle horse could catch up with Ida's buggy horse without too much trouble."

I could imagine Lucas doing exactly that.

My editor came back and settled into her chair.

"He caught up with the buggy horse, reached down and grabbed the harness, but the horse reared up and jerked Lucas sideways. He lost his balance and fell. Amy, Lucas fell under the buggy. He got dragged beneath it!"

I could no longer breathe. I think my heart stopped. I jumped up from the table and shouted into the phone. "Is he still alive?"

My editor's jaw dropped. Other diners stopped eating and stared at me. A server hurried toward me. I waved him off as I headed toward the front of the hotel, my editor following closely behind.

"He is alive, but he's hurt bad. Internal bleeding they almost didn't find in time. A concussion—he hasn't regained consciousness yet. Three broken ribs. One of his arms is broken. He's on life support."

My editor hurried along beside me, a worried expression on her face.

"Where is he now, Erma?" I asked.

"They life-flighted him to Cleveland Clinic. He's in their trauma unit."

I stopped moving when I got outside the hotel, trying to focus on how to get to Lucas as quickly as possible. Doormen stood about.

Tourists took pictures of one another. Horns honked and traffic noisily swept by.

"I'll be there as soon as I can, Erma."

"You're coming to Sugarcreek?"

"Of course not. I'm going to Cleveland. Who is with him"

"Samuel is with him," Erma said.

"That's good."

"You forgot this." My editor shoved my purse into my hand. "We'll finish talking about your next project later."

I nodded my thanks. A taxi drove by. I waved it down.

"Where to, lady?" The driver asked.

I gave him my address. As I climbed into the taxi, the thing that struck me the strongest was how incredibly unimportant my work felt right now compared to the fact that doctors were fighting for Lucas's life.

Although I had never been a particularly religious person, a desperate plea *"Father God! Don't let him die!"* formed in my mind and began repeating itself over and over like a drumbeat that was perfectly aligned with the pounding of my heart.

The End
(for now)

AUTHOR'S NOTE

I've always been fascinated by the Amish—their commitment to community, family, and faith offers a striking contrast to our modern, disconnected world. Writing this story allowed me to explore what happens when these two worlds collide through Amy and Lucas.

This novel asks: What makes a family? Is it blood, shared beliefs, or simply the people who show up when you need them most?

For Amy, discovering her unexpected heritage forces her to reconcile unique pieces of herself, much like mismatched quilt squares that ultimately create something beautiful.

I hope you enjoyed spending time with these characters as much as I did creating them. Their journey continues in the next book, and I can't wait to share it with you.

PENNSYLVANIA DUTCH GLOSSARY

Holmes County Deitsch is largely an oral tradition with few official written standards. As such, spellings used in the glossary aim to reflect pronunciation and usage, not standardized orthography. Variation among speakers is natural and expected.

Ach - Oh; an exclamation
Alle - All
Awwright - All right
Bischt du awwright? - Are you all right?
Blumen - Flowers
Boppli - Baby
Brieder – Brothers
Bu - Boy
Daadi Haus - Grandfather house; smaller dwelling on Amish property for older family members
Daett - Father/Dad
Danki/Denki - Thank you
Die kinner - The children
Erde - Earth, soil
Gewiss net - Certainly not
Glaeder - Clothes
Gude - Good
Gut - Good
Gviss - Certain, definitely
Haus - House
Ich will hame zu mei kinner - I want to go home to my children
Ja - Yes
Komm schnell - Come quickly
Kummer rei - Come in
Kumm - Come
Meedlies - Girls
Mamm - Mother/Mom
Mann - Man, husband
Mei sohn - My son
Nee - No
Net - Not
Recht - Right, correct

Schweschder - Sister
Sei brav - Be good
Wort - Word
Wo war's - Where was it?

SNEAK PEEK

SECRETS OF SUGARCREEK 3

THE QUIET SOLDIER

Cleveland Clinic
July

My reflection in the darkened hospital window startled me—hair disheveled, eyes hollow with fatigue and fear, my clothes so rumpled, I might as well have been wearing rags. I'd never looked worse or cared less.

It's amazing how terror can clarify the mind and re-organize priorities.

After driving white-knuckled for seven hours from my home in Manhattan, I stepped into the Cleveland Clinic's emergency department, my heart pounding. The antiseptic smell hit me like an invisible wall—that peculiar hospital mixture of cleaning products and something medicinal that never quite masked the underlying scent of human suffering.

Ten weeks I had been gone, determined to give Lucas the space to find his Amish bride without having to watch and ache while he did so. Now here I was, racing back at the first word of his accident, every mile between New York and Ohio a blur.

I approached a gray-haired volunteer who wore a fluffy pink cardigan against the chill of the hospital, and a name tag that read "Maude."

"I'm looking for Lucas Hershberger." I tightly gripped the counter with my fingers. "I'm told he was brought in here."

"Oh, yes," the woman, said, typing something into the computer. "The Amish boy. Such a shame."

"Wait, what?" My heart felt like it had dropped into my shoes. "What do you mean? He's still alive, isn't he?"

"As far as I know," she said, with haste. "He's been transferred to the Neuro Intensive Care Unit.

"What does that mean?"

"That's where they take someone with severe head injuries, dear." Her voice held too much sympathy. It frightened me.

I glanced around. "Just tell me how to get there."

She gave me the instructions. When I finally reached the Neuro ICU, the waiting room was filled with Lucas's Amish friends and family. A sea of black hats and bonnets greeted me, their old-fashioned clothing, a stark contrast to the hospital's sterile modernism.

They made room for me, politely, even though the light-colored linen slacks and silk blouse I'd been wearing when Erma called, marked me as an outsider as clearly as if I'd worn a flashing neon sign.

"You came!" My Amish neighbor, Erma, rose from her chair and approached me. She was a rosy-cheeked woman who usually spent her days tending her flowers, baking cookies for her grandchildren, and laughing at their antics. Except today she wasn't laughing. She wasn't even smiling. Her eyes were red-rimmed, and she clutched a crumpled handkerchief.

I'd never seen her look this solemn.

"How is he?" My voice was strained as I forced words around the lump in my throat.

"Still unconscious. They have him on life support. They say the next forty-eight hours are critical."

Seeing the stricken look on my face, she tried to reassure me.

"Lucas is a strong man." She glanced at the group of Amish people standing behind her, watching our exchange. "And we have been praying."

I nodded, no longer trusting myself to speak. I was relatively ignorant of most things religious, but at this moment, I hoped with all my heart that there was a compassionate God listening to these people's prayers.

Lucas's mother, Naomi, approached, her face etched with worry but her bearing dignified. "*Danki* for coming," she said. "Lucas will be pleased to see you when he wakes."

'When' not 'if.' The simple faith in her words nearly undid me.

"Is anyone with him?" I managed.

"His father," Naomi replied. "For now, they are only allowing one visitor at a time and only immediate family."

I glanced toward the double doors that separated the waiting area from the patient rooms. I ached to push through them, to verify with my own eyes that he was still alive.

"Amy has traveled a long way," Erma said, her tone careful. "Perhaps she could see him briefly when Albert comes out."

I shot Erma a grateful look.

The thought of Lucas lying silent and unresponsive twisted inside me. Lucas, who could calm a skittish horse with a few words, who described the discovery of a hummingbird nest with awe, who carried his tiny niece to school on his broad shoulders every morning so she wouldn't have to struggle to keep up with the other children.

Naomi hesitated. I could tell that her inherent kindness at war with her need to follow hospital rules.

I didn't want her to have to make that choice. Her life was too hard already. There was nothing I could do for Lucas. I knew my desire to see him rested entirely upon my own need.

"It's okay," I said. "I'll wait."

The relief on Naomi's face was palpable as I sank into a chair. I sat slightly apart from the group, conscious of being the outsider—the *Englisch* woman who didn't belong in this circle of shared faith and blood ties.

Although everyone spoke English when they addressed me, they all lapsed into Pennsylvania Deutsch when they talked to one another.

Samuel, Lucas's brother-in-law, approached, carrying a paper cup of coffee, and handed it to me.

I took the coffee and thanked him, grateful for his thoughtfulness. "How are Gretchen and the girls?"

"The unborn babe, and our three little daughters are well and growing. My wife is anxious about her brother, but thought it best to keep the girls at home. Her ankles have been swelling, so the midwife advised against her traveling right now. And a hospital waiting room is not the best place for small *kinder*."

"True," I agreed. "This sort of thing is hard on children. It's not a great place for grownups, either."

"Also true." He looked at me with sympathy, his head cocked to one side. "Unless you cannot bear to be anywhere else?"

My throat grew tight at his understanding.

People from their family and community continued to arrive until there were not enough chairs for everyone. As one of the younger people there, I gave up my seat and curled myself against the wall near an electrical outlet, taking the opportunity to recharge my phone and laptop. Some of his people stretched out on the floor. No one left. No one spoke of getting a hotel for the night. As I waited through the night, the fluorescent lights in the ceiling kept buzzing like angry bees.

Lucas Hershberger — my neighbor, my friend, my impossible heartache — lay somewhere behind the double doors of the trauma ward, battered and broken. I sat on the floor with my back against the wall while my mind ran around in frantic circles.

Hours passed. Whispered Pennsylvania Dutch conversations

ebbed and flowed around me like water around a stone. The steady beeping of monitors occasionally drifted through when the doors to the patient area opened. Each time, my heart would leap, hoping for news about Lucas.

ALSO BY SERENA B. MILLER

ALSO BY SERENA B. MILLER

ABOUT THE AUTHOR

SERENA B. MILLER is a power-house in both publishing and television, earning her place as a *USA Today Bestselling Author* and collecting prestigious honors including the Romance Writers of America **RITA**, the American Christian Fiction Writers **CAROL**, and recognition as a **CHRISTY** Award finalist. Her signature storytelling first leaped from page to screen when *The Sugar Haus Inn* from her *Love's Journey in Sugarcreek* series became the award-winning UPTV movie *Love Finds You in Sugarcreek*, capturing the coveted **Templeton Epiphany Award**. Her mastery of heartfelt narratives has since inspired two acclaimed Hallmark Channel features: the compelling *An Uncommon Grace* and the captivating *Moriah's Lighthouse*, the latter drawn from her *Love's Journey on Manitoulin Island* series and set against the stunning backdrop of coastal France.

For More Information, Please visit serenabmiller.com

facebook.com/AuthorSerenaMiller

x.com/Serenabmiller

instagram.com/serenabmiller

amazon.com/author/serenabmiller

bookbub.com/authors/serena-b-miller

goodreads.com/SerenaBMiller